GW00401383

Copyright © 2020 High One Anthology Happy London Press
All Images ©CNewton2020
The copyright of each writer's work remains the sole property
of the contributing writer and the copyright in this anthology
"as a collective work" belongs to the anthology publisher
Happy London Press.

All rights reserved.

First Published November 2020
ISBN 978-1-912951-60-4
Limited Edition Hardback

No part of this book may be reproduced in any form or
by any electronic or mechanical means, including information
storage and retrieval systems, without written permission from the
author, except for the use of brief quotations in a book review.

Artist Prints and cards are available to purchase
HappyStoryStore.com

HAPPY LONDON PRESS
Independent publishing for new talented authors
Happylondonpress.com

HappyLDNPress@gmail.com

Come and join our chatty community,
fun events or become a beta-reader

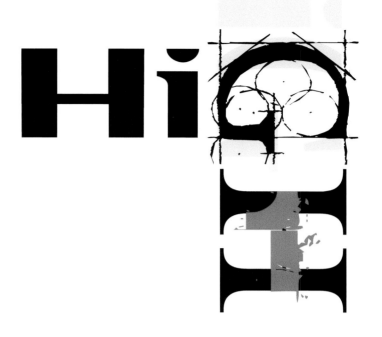

Photographic Art
Clare Newton FRSA

A prize-winning collection
of short stories from new writers

PROLOGUE *by* ALEXANDRA ELY

❝ It is a writer's dream of seeing their stories on the shelves of bookstores and Happy London Press has provided a means for making such dreams come true. HI2020 Short Story Competition was set up to allow the opportunity for new writers to shine.

As it turned out, the competition also became something to look forward to during the COVID19 pandemic and lockdown. It certainly gave me something to anticipate during those slow quarantine months. I was delighted when HLP asked me to be the international judge for the competition. As one of the five top tier judges, the stories I received were colourful, unpredictable and the variety was thrilling.

Quarter finalist stories were divided among the five top tier judges to select one each for the five finalists, from which the very best contest winner was chosen from hundreds of entries. I commend all the writers for their hard work and dedication to this craft. This anthology holds mystery, heartbreak, adventure, romance, and the bizarre and the creativity each story is rich and entertaining. There is a genre in the compilation to suit all kinds of readers, in this beautifully illustrated coffee-table-read to engage your mind and tickle your fancy.

Although this year has been fraught with Covid disappointments, this book shines as a beacon of light in the lives of these now published writers and it is hoped will bring enlightenment to you too. Please drop in a review and share links where you purchase this book, it makes such a difference to the writers. ❞

Alexandra

Alexandra Ely
Top Tier Judge USA

So many winning short stories from Hi 2020!

thE eAGLE CAfE

BY KAYLEIGH MADDOCKS

The day is too hot to be considered
comfortable. I walk up the stone steps to
the front door of the Oakwood Nursing
Home, papers clutched in my hand.
"I'm here from the university,"
I tell the woman on the desk,
"...to read to the residents."

WITHOUT GLANCING AT ME, SHE POINTS her perfectly manicured hands down the corridor....I count the rooms as I go, ducking into 106. An old man is sitting out on his balcony, a carer helping him eat.

I introduce myself and sit down opposite him. I am not sure he is lucid enough to understand, but it is what I am here to do, so I flatten the papers out on my lap and begin.

2262. I was in the final year of university. Time travel was old hat by that time. It was not deemed manageable for nine billion people to have free rein of the past, so it had been reserved for final year students. I had worked hard for the top spot, so I could have five jumps instead of the standard four.

The assignment was simple; pick a time-period and critically analyse the culture of the day. Easy.

"Do not speak to anyone. Do not try to change anything. Do not get involved in any politics. Everson, I'm talking to you," Mr Blois, our short and ill-tempered history master had told us, "and no, you can't kill Hitler." How we had laughed.

At lunch we spoke over each other as we laid out our plans. "I think I'll do my essay on the French Revolution," Emmett Everson had said as he chewed on a peach.

"I'm going to Ancient Greece," piped up Leonie Gray.

"What about you, Elis?" Rowan Webb had asked me.

A grin spread over my face, "1984."

Something about the nineteen-eighties had always fascinated me. I had pored over history books, learning about the miners' strikes, Margaret Thatcher, and, Oh, the clothes! My friends had wanted to attend grand coronations, dance in the roaring twenties, or walk with the Egyptians. Not me.

"What happened in 1984?" asked Emmett, his pudgy face screwed quite ungainly.

"Life."

The day of the jump, my class gathered in the main hall. The myriad of costumes made for quite a sight. Some in togas, some in camouflage. Gerry Baitlin was dressed like a gladiator. I had swept my crimped hair to the side and bought some replica high-top boots. I wore red high-waisted three-quarter length trousers and a garish yellow off the shoulder shirt that was littered with geometric shapes. I looked amazing.

I strapped the cuff-like device to my wrist as Mr Blois told us, "punch in the numbers on the keypad, wait for the light to go green. On return, the device will flash orange and beep three times before you are pulled back. You have six hours."

The clock struck twelve, and we all eagerly entered our designated years. I blinked, and in a moment, I was in the middle of a busy highway.

Cars whipped past me as I fought to keep my balance. I ran to the side, breathing hard. Steadying myself, I looked closer at the automobiles. They seemed a little wrong. Did they have Triumph Roadsters in 1984?

I walked briskly, turning left into a street full of shops. The fashions seemed dated. I wanted the famed Oxford Street. Though there could be a degree of error, it was time travel after all. Shaking my head, I tried to focus, as people had gawked.

Eager to get off the street, I beeline'd for the nearest building, an old indoor market. It was two stories, with a glass roof casting sunlight down over the rows of shops. The wrought iron railings of the upper balcony were covered in thick green Christmas decorations, and a large tree sat in the centre of the market.

More stares followed as I pushed through the throngs, and I ducked into a glass fronted café. In my haste, I walked straight into the server, making him tip his tray down himself. Coffee and two chocolate eclairs cascaded down our legs.

I looked up at his face and was lost in his apologies. His accent was thick, and his eyes a brilliant green. His black curls were cut smartly. Taking my hand, he led me to a vacant table.

"Are you OK?" he asked, offering me a worn tea towel to wipe the coffee from my legs. I knew I couldn't talk to him, so I just politely nodded, setting my mouth to a thin line.

Looking around, I saw the café was empty. Two people sat perched on the other side of the large window, though their afternoon tea now incomplete. A peeling poster was haphazardly stuck to the side of the counter.

Celebrate New Year's 1949 at the Eagle Café. 1949?

"What year is it?" I asked the man before I could stop myself. His eyes narrowed as he laughed, "1948, Miss."

I rubbed my forehead and sighed deeply, in my eagerness I must have got the last two numbers the wrong way round. This was frustrating. It certainly explained stares. At least I had started with one more visit than my cohort, now we would be on equal footing.

When I had stopped wallowing, the man, who introduced himself as Luca Ricci, brought over two cups of hot chocolate. I had no means to pay, but he told me it was on the house for tipping the tray, though in truth that had been my fault.

We laughed heartily as we swapped stories of family and of life, though mine were obviously muted. He told me he was from Italy; his mother had moved to England during the war after his father had been killed.

As the device on my wrist beeped and I excused myself, he asked me would I meet him again. I nodded, though I had no intention of ever returning to 1948.

And technically that was true because the next time I jumped I went to 1949. My classmates had bragged about witnessing Cleopatra or King Henry VIII in action, but I was lost in daydreams of grey London and a little café in the East End.

My heart swooped when I saw him, and we had hot chocolate on the bank of the Thames. In 1950, he took me dancing on my birthday. I promised I would see him on Christmas Eve. He was taking me to the Ritz.

As I jumped, rain pounded the pavement so hard it rebounded up the legs of the mindless masses making their way home.

Crossing the street, I turned into the emporium. It looked different, must have had a coat of paint over the summer. The market inside was busy with people poring over stalls and through shops for the perfect festive gifts.

I searched the teeming teashop for Luca. I spied a spot at an empty table and slid into the booth. Tapping the table mindlessly, I hardly noticed the older man dropping into the seat opposite me.

"Oh, I'm sorry," I said to him, noticing the two steaming mugs in his hands, "I'm waiting for a friend."

Then I noticed his eyes. Bright green. Luca's father maybe, though he told me he was long dead. And then realisation crashed over me. Luca offered me the saddest of smiles. The calendar behind his head read 1988.

"Sorry I'm late," I murmur.

We sat there for hours, long after the last customer had left. He told me about his life. He had married eventually, and his daughters helped him in the café. He pointed them out, two beautiful girls around my age. They both had his eyes. He showed me photos of his grandchildren.

My heart was heavy, grief gripped me. I could go back; I had one more jump left. I could go to 1950, unclip the device and live a long and happy life with the man in front of me. But then the people he loved would not exist. His daughters and grandchildren would never be born. I was not prepared to ask that of him.

As the device on my wrist beeped, Luca gripped my hand.

"Will I see you again?" he asked, whispering something in my ear as I faded.

— ~ —

I look up and see he is listening as best he can. The carer, Janine, is watching me, patiently waiting for more.

I lean in, dropping a kiss onto his cheek. A tear escapes me. "Ti amo," I whisper, as the twinkle in his old green eyes extinguishes.

Janine rushes to him, her fingers seeking a pulse on his wrist. As she turns to ask me to get help, there is nothing more than the echo of the last beep left behind.

"That's all of it," I smile at her.

ROUGH JUSTICE

BY BOB THOMPSON

Murder is never a good start to a day. I was
just sipping my morning coffee and tucking
into my croissant when the call came in.
They had called responders to a shop on the
Broadway after gunfire was heard.

They had found a body...

THE SHOP HAD NOT BEEN BUSY. Mrs Singh had been putting out tubs of yoghurt into the refrigerated cabinet at the back. Old man Riley had been reading the front pages, which he did every morning and Daisy Walters had been by the confectionery looking for chocolate.

Singh knew about all these things because every aisle of his tiny shop was covered by CCTV linked to a display behind the counter. Every ten seconds a different camera. I found it mesmeric.

Singh was always expecting trouble. He kept a cricket bat behind the counter for just such an eventuality. He kept all the valuable stock – the cigarettes, the alcohol – behind the toughened glass security screen.

It was all very familiar. In my mind's eye, I saw the baggy jeans, the hoodies and the swagger that says, "Don't mess with me." I knew it for what it was – lads looking to steal alcohol or cigarettes. Usually, it was knives that were the problem.

At what point the gun was produced, I had yet to establish. I had a clear picture of events, thanks mainly to Daisie's observational skills. I had tried talking to Mrs. Singh, but she was in too much of a state. Frank Riley had been taken to hospital. His attempts to intervene had proved too much.

Daisy had identified them readily enough – Damien Hancock and his brother – and I had them picked up. I knew Damien. He was an unpleasant character involved in thieving and drugs. Guns had once been out of his league, but now? It was time Damien saw some justice.

I had the gun. It had been dropped in their haste to escape. It was an odd one, a revolver, battered – still lethal. I guessed that it had been stolen–they wouldn't have had money to buy it.

Back at the station, someone raised the prospect of a racial motive. The youths had attempted to hold up the shop when the owner refused to play ball. They shot him. The last thing I wanted was people crawling all over the case waving the race card.

The news that Frank Riley had died just made it worse. According to Daisy, Frank had tackled one of them before they fled. I blenched at the thought of a ninety-year-old lashing out at an armed villain, but my commercial instincts soon kicked in. I rang my contact at the news desk.

"Usual rate?" "Of course."

Butler in forensics had been doing his job almost as long as I had. "The bullet shattered the glass screen before hitting the victim in the middle of his chest, passing through his heart. It was quick – he wouldn't have suffered."

"I am sure that will give his relatives some comfort. What about the murder weapon?"

"Ah, interesting, a Webley, must be fifty years old. We used to see more of them. Army people forgot to return them when they were demobbed. It is a forty-five calibre, which makes it more of a cannon than a pistol. No prints, only smudges. I may help on its origins. I have a contact who works for the manufacturer. This beast has a serial number. They may tell us its history and help you nail the nasty bastard that pulled the trigger."

It had proved easy to apprehend Damien Hancock. He was at home when uniform came knocking. When I returned from the morgue he was waiting with the duty solicitor. I grabbed DS Davis and went to see the little shit. He was sitting back, trying to appear nonchalant. While we were setting up he yawned loudly.

Davis began, "Can we start with your whereabouts at eight-thirty this morning?"

"A bit early for me. I was in bed"

"At home?"

"Yes. At home"

"Can anybody vouch for that? Girlfriend? Boyfriend?"

Davis had touched the intended nerve, "Are you saying I am gay?"

"The problem is Damien" I paused and took a sip of water. Pace is everything in extracting a confession. "We have witnesses that put you in Singhs Supermarket at eight-thirty with your brother."

He became warier "I don't know nothing about that. You can't put that on me." "Put what on you Damien?"

"He got shot, they say. It wasn't nothing to do with me."

"Singh was murdered, Damien. You know that the shop has CCTV?" "Gentlemen" the solicitor intervened "May I have time alone with my client?"

I watched them through the one-way mirror. The cockiness was gone, nervousness breaking out into bouts of agitation. "We've got him," said Davis "and he knows it. We just need to hear it from him. There is no CCTV footage. The hard disk broke a couple of months ago, and the son says his father was too tight to get it fixed. All it does is display."

"Fuck" The watertight case I had imagined had sprung a leak. "Have his clothes been sent to Forensics?"

When we returned Damien was sitting on the edge of his seat.

"My client would like to make a statement" the solicitor announced.

"I was at Singhs Supermarket this morning. I went to buy beer. Normally he isn't too fussy about ID. This time he wanted me to prove I was old enough. We got into a row about it. He was shouting at me. Then this guy crashed into me and there was an explosion. We ran for it."

"Thank you, Damien" he appeared pleased.

"When did you draw the gun?" Davis went straight for the jugular

His smile was replaced with confusion. "What gun? I don't have a gun."

A knock at the door interrupted the interrogation. In the corridor outside the duty Sergeant handed me an email. "From Forensics," he hissed, "His jacket sleeve is covered in residue. The CPS is happy to proceed."

I re-entered the room and terminated the interview. "Damien Hancock. Having reviewed the evidence both I am satisfied that we have passed the necessary thresholds. You will be charged with the murder of Hardeep Singh. Sergeant Davis will read you your rights."

The solicitor shrugged. Damien, in denial, kept repeating "No" as I left the room.

Someone had brought in the evening paper. Blazoned across the front page was "Have a go hero dies" I skimmed through the article. The reporter had contacted Frank Riley's daughter. Apparently, he was a major and had fought in Korea. Who knew?

A hearing saw Damien remanded in custody alongside his brother with a trial set a couple of months away. Both of them still denied everything, but the residue was damning. The consensus was that they were going down for murder.

A few weeks on and my focus had switched onto other cases allocated to my team. I was planning on a quiet drink when I came across Butler in the bar. We chatted about the kids, our golf handicaps, and caught up on life away from the blue light. Butler brought up the gun used to kill Singh.

"Finally, I heard from my contact. That serial number was issued to the Gloucestershire regiment in 1950. I don't know if that helps."

Far from helping, it raised a nagging doubt in my mind. Back in the office, I pulled out the Singh file. There, among all the things that didn't make it to the official record, was a photocopy of the front page the day Frank Riley appeared.

I soon found what I was looking for. Details of his service record. I had been correct to feel uneasy about the provenance of the gun. Frank Riley had been a Major in the Gloucestershire Regiment.

There is an easy fiction that policing exists to investigate criminality and not judge right and wrong. In fact, such decisions are made constantly in assumptions we make and the trajectories we take in any investigation. Inconvenient facts can be put down to coincidence and ignored in the pursuit of what is right.

Damien's defence all along had been that the old man had attacked him. If the gun has been fired in close proximity, they have showered Damien in residue whether he pulled the trigger. I could hear a barrister picking away at my case.

Frank had probably held onto the gun when he left the army. Would it be right to tarnish his reputation with a manslaughter charge? He was a hero.

The probability was that Damien had fired the gun – anything else was just speculation. The shredder buzzed as the document disappeared along with my memory

After all, Dam

YOU CARRY IT

BY MARIAM VARSIMASHVILI

His lips glitches into a contorted smile.
"Do you have enough supplies?",
he asked. I lifted my giant bowl of thick
noodles to the camera.

The only things left at the supermarket
were shining packets of instant soup.
I had organised the sachets of spices in
order of my preference...

I REPLAYED THE LAST PUBLIC GATHERING over and over in my head; a parade of blushing boys, dressed in baby blue and pink cone-hats, decorated with frills of white lace. Their heads were bandaged as if they had all been in a car crash. They paced around in long frocks that matched their hats, blowing whistles and throwing tangerines at each other.

Three months before, Jake began displaying peculiar symptoms; blood-shot eyes, flesh that was hardening like clay and peeling off like snake's skin, preparing to enlarge his pores for the features, we still weren't sure what he was going to be. His shrinking mouth frequently coughed up bristles that flew off in the sky like helium balloons.

In the first week, he completely depended on me humming through the microphone, administering virtual affection. His eyes hadn't opened yet. I guided him to food that was dropped off on his porch; a pouch of cockroaches, beetles, spiders and small snails. Despite the nutrition, he tired easily and stayed huddled near to the laptop.

When the virus spread more quickly than predicted, the government offered the simple advice of staying at home, avoiding contact with animals. In a few weeks' time, the cherry blossoms sprouting in masses had no audience to admire them. They fell on the pavements, waiting for the wind to sweep them away onto empty roads.

Hospitals became overwhelmed. The dozens printed images of vets bruised from the imprint of their masks. They placed all pets in isolation units. Some owners, wanting to spare them a lonely life, handed their pets to a pair of yellow gloves that locked them in cages in the back of large trucks and sent them to the slaughterhouse. A photograph of a woman lying limp on her horse's back went viral. The virus had turned her ebony hair to strawberry blonde and transformed her feet into stumpy hooves.

After Jake started displaying some symptoms of flu, we joked and guessed what kind of animal he would metamorphose into. The next time I phoned him, he refused to let me see his face. I focused the camera on his hands that cupped a glass of water. I could hear him sobbing.

After a short while, he was going to be a bird. Nobody knew if, after the change, the mind still functioned as normal. Scientists were working tirelessly to find not only a cure, but a way to communicate with the survivors. Jake feared being incomprehensible.

Soon, he developed pin feathers on his back. Tube-like growths that, according to the internet, would eventually pan out into fully developed wings. His eyes enlarged, taking over most of his face. They darted around on my computer screen, unable to stay still. His fingers became webbed and he found it increasingly difficult to speak. He took longer to answer my questions, leaving huge gaps between words.

"I love you", I told him.

The death toll rose by two percent each week.

I had been quarantined with my mother for months. She died a few weeks before Jake started transitioning, her last words to me being: "Make sure you wash your hands every ten minutes, as if you just peeled jalapenos and want to replace your contact lenses." I wrapped her up in our Persian rug and dug a simple grave in the garden. I put geraniums on top of the soil.

Jake, except for a few patches of bare skin on his head and face, was covered in white feathers. He perched on his chair, tapping the camera with his beak and squawking. He had a scruffy appearance, but from the look in his eyes, I knew he was still conscious.

During this stage, he flapped his feathers uncontrollably. I read him James Joyce's Ulysses; a book Jake had always wanted to finish. The bird stared into the camera lens as if it understood every word.

"Jake, are you still there?"

On good days, he lifted his wings or tapped the screen in response to my question. On bad days, he stared into the lens unknowingly, indifferent to the sound of my voice.

Soon, he became impatient with my reading. Instead, he seemed eager to show off his new skill; fluttering and hopping on the table, raising his wings higher than he had ever done before. He strained his neck and bending down; he picked at the strange spotting on his feathery body that distinguished him from other swans.

Despite the companies I worked for going bankrupt, I continued to make illustrations. I drew a woman recovering old parsnips from the back of her fridge and incorporating them into her cooking. I drew my mother sitting on the couch, knitting a red sweater. I drew Jake. His old body, human and hairy. I drew the line of shoppers waiting at the back of supermarkets, some of them half-transformed, sporting snouts and tails. Mostly, I drew people eating junk food. Large burgers that oozed grease and ketchup, fries dipped in vanilla milkshake, glazed chicken thighs, tacos drizzled with guacamole and salsa, dribbling down strangers' mouths. I drew a group of girls in their pyjamas, eating pepperoni pizza on a fluffy, pink carpet. One was caught in a web of mozzarella cheese.

As his transition reached its peak, Jake's behaviour became more unpredictable. He seemed aggravated by his surroundings and frequently attacked the screen. Because of the damage, I could only see him through linear cracks. He spread his wings, lined with arrows of feathers, and flew around his living room. I still read Ulysses and pretended he was listening. One day he knocked over the laptop during his flight. I couldn't see Jake anymore, instead I stared at a bowl of rotting fruit. Sometimes I'd hear the tapping of his feet in the background.

I kept phoning and talking with him until the tapping sound disappeared and I was met with a single loose feather balancing on an infested apple.

I don't know what happened to Jake. I can only assume that he found a way out and flew away. Before I shut my laptop down, I illustrated the new Jake, living in some lake or wetland, wobbling awkwardly on land, using his long and flexible neck to grab shoots in shallow waters.

I was down to my last sachet of instant soup, mushroom and chicken. My least favourite. I went to the toilet and realised that I hadn't looked at myself for months. I could see the outline of my features more starkly than before. A few thick hairs had sprouted on my upper lip and chin. I put the shower on and lifted my yellow shirt over my head, unsurprised to see the fuzzy black and white stripes covering every inch of skin.

Thank God I Didn't

BY ALAN RAFFERTY

There are times in your life when
you think, "I wish I had..."
And there are times when you
think, "Thank God I didn't..."
This was the latter...

THURSDAY, NOVEMBER 14TH, 1974, COVENTRY.

I was rushing down to the school hall. I had volunteered to stay late to show the parents of potential school entrants for the following year around. I had done so for one reason only. Rosemary had volunteered. Boys were expected to escort girls home as we were late leaving, and I hoped that a long shot would give me the chance to escort Rosemary home. I had ridden my bike to school to make this possible.

Rosemary and I had been sitting next to each other in registration for five years. It started because everyone else had paired off in the first term and we were the two left over. Initially, it was inertia that kept us next to each other (and a lack of desks), but we started talking at registration. It wasn't until we went into sixth form that I suddenly realised how much I enjoyed this time and how I felt about Rosemary. All the boys went for Kate, who had more obvious attractions for a teenage boy. I pretended to like their smutty jokes about her, but really they made me sick. Rosemary is the only one for me. She may not be so obviously attractive, but there is a beauty about her that cannot be defined. Added to that, she has deep brown eyes you could drown in, a smile that would light up the darkest night, and a gentle infectious laugh that included rather than mocked.

When I arrived at the hall, my heart dropped. Jane was there. Jane, an ardent feminist, came from near me. I was asked to escort Jane home. Jane had short blond hair, blue eyes, and a demeanor that gave the impression that she would have fitted in well in the Gestapo. Her aspiration was to become a motorbike courier in the WRNS. I spent as much time as I could that evening, duties permitting, talking to Rosemary, trying to pluck up the courage to ask her to the sixth form Christmas Party. I knew I failed when I wasn't asked to escort Jane home.

"I don't need an escort," she said through gritted teeth.

Knowing better than to let our headmaster, a former army major, hear her question his decision. In truth, she didn't. She was far more capable of looking after herself than I was. We left for home, Jane walking and me pushing my bike.

"Just to let you know that I don't need an escort and wouldn't have chosen you even if I did. Just to let you know that I wanted to escort Rosemary not an idiot like you."

"Oh, we're hot on Rosemary...", she stopped short as she saw me redden.

Our route took us close to the city centre. At the council house we turned right and at St Mary's Lane, Jane sneered, "If you want to go I can perfectly manage from here." I carried on walking with her. At Bayley Lane she gave me another chance, but I carried on with her. It was not because I wanted to, but because I had said I would escort her home and, to me, giving my word was as good as a promise.

As we passed the Herbert Museum and Art Gallery, we heard a loud thud. We turned to see if there had been a crash but could see nothing. Moments later a man came running from the direction of the Cathedral and banged into me and then smacked into the pavement entangled with my bike. It was typical that it was Jane who took the belligerent stance. But the man picked himself up and just kept running. We continued on. At the top of Jane's road, near Coventry City grounds at Highfield Road, I finally got so fed up with the jip Jane was giving me that I cycled off home, leaving her.

I woke up determined to find some time to ask Rosemary to go with me to the party. I got ready for school and was eating breakfast before going for the bus when the front doorbell went. My dad answered it and came back with two policemen. "What have you been up to?", said my dad.

"We'll handle this if you don't mind, Sir. John, we understand that you were walking through the city centre last night."

"Yes. I was escorting Jane home after we were late from school."

"Your girlfriend?"

"Not likely, not her. Boys are expected to escort girls home if we are late. Neither of us liked the arrangement."

"Did you hear anything, or anything happen?"

"Well, we heard a thud like a lorry crash, but then again not. Then a guy came running from the direction of the Cathedral and banged into us. Then he ran off."

"Could you tell us what he looked like?'

"Sorry it was too dark, and I was nursing a bruised and scraped shin. Jane got a better look at him."

"Jane has given us a description already. Your story corroborates hers. What were you wearing last night?"

"My school uniform, of course."

"What you are wearing now?"

"Yes."

"I am sorry, but we are going to have to take your clothes and bike away with us for forensic examination. Can you get changed, please. You will have to come with us too, as we will need to eliminate anything on your clothes or bike from you."

I got up to get changed and the police officer's radio beeped. He spoke into it and then listened.

"Seems that the man who bumped into you has come forward as a witness, so no need for any forensic examination. Thank you for your time. However, please stay at home today and don't try to contact Jane or anyone else from your school. We have informed your school."

It was only when we read the morning paper that we found out that there had been an IRA bomb in Coventry that night. About four that afternoon, they lifted my curfew. November 16th. I was standing in the old cathedral ruins, looking at the police cordon on the other side of the road. I had been standing there for an hour. There was nothing to see of the bomb or its consequences but, somehow, I couldn't break at the intended target as a Fusilier service here in the cathedral. A hand reached out and squeezed my right hand.

I automatically squeezed back, thankful for the comfort it gave me, and the hand stayed there in mine. "I knew that I would find you here. You always come here when you are troubled." It was Rosemary's voice.

"Coincidence."

"Jane was giving me so much angst Thursday night that I almost left her and came down Bayley Lane past here to go home. It could have been so close."

"Thank God you didn't." Something in her voice made me turn. There were tears in her eyes. I took her right hand in my left and we stood looking at each other, hands held for mutual comfort. Then she broke her hands away, only to put them on my shoulders and kiss me on the cheek.

I moved my hands to rest them on her hips. Suddenly she threw her arms round my neck and gripped so tightly that I thought she would break it. She gave me a kiss like I had never had before, nor dreamed could even be possible. How could she put such desperation, passion and love into a single kiss? She pulled back smiling, arms still round my neck. I moved my hands up her back and moved in for another kiss. I did not want it to end. Eventually it had to.

"How did you know?", I asked.

"Jane rang me. She was worried about you, but whatever you do, don't let on you know. It would ruin her hard girl image. Now it is time you walked me home."

It perplexed me. It was only three in the afternoon. "Well, if you are going to take me to the Christmas party, know where I live so you can pick me up, don't you?" We both laughed. She had always made me laugh. Rosemary turned to go, still holding my right hand, but allowed me one last glance back.

"Yes", I thought, "Thank God, I didn't."

The Ballad of Billy the Kid

BY SHERRY HOSTLER

Today was going to be the day. Will knew this as soon as his battered old clock radio started playing The Boomtown Rats at 6.00am. He didn't need to be up that early to go to school, but today was a big day as he had to get ready for his Year 9 presentation at assembly.

HE'D BEEN WORKING ON IT FOR AGES NOW, and at last he was going to have a captive audience. He didn't especially like getting up in the mornings these days, especially Monday mornings. It would be far easier to just stay in bed, with the curtains pulled protectively against the rest of the world. Easier to pretend that he was safe and nothing had ever changed.

Some days Will would lie in his cocoon and think about the younger version of himself. He could still remember what it was like to throw off his duvet in the morning and leap out of bed as soon as the first crack of light peered cheekily around the side of his Toy Story curtains. He'd always been eager to start the day back then no matter what lay ahead. Each new morning was like the unwrapping of a gift, and the curiosity of his tender years wanted to embrace it with enthusiasm.

The best days were always those when his older brother was around to play with. There were only three years between them, but to Will it appeared Jacob had a lifetime of worldly wisdom, and he was the person that Will wanted to be like the most when he grew up.

Will's favourite game in the world to play with his brother was Cowboys and Indians. Jacob always made out that he was far too old for such silliness, but Will knew that deep down he loved it just as much as he did.

"Do we have to play this stupid game again, Will?" He'd ask, huffing and puffing while digging out his old cowboy hat and toy gun. By this time Will's hopeful face would already be adorned with warrior stripes courtesy of his mum's waxy red lipstick, his feathered headdress tickling the back of his neck.

It was the most fun thing ever for Will, and even though he never got to be the cowboy, he still enjoyed dressing up like a Red Indian Chief. Clutching his plastic bow and arrow set to his skinny little chest, he would shout Apache war cries until his dad yelled for him to keep the flaming noise down.

On rainy days, the game turned into hide and seek inside the house. Will would scamper off on his make believe horse, leaving Jacob to count to ten before shouting "Coming to find those pesky Injuns!"

Holed away under a bed or behind the overstuffed lounge furniture, Will would try to breathe as quietly as possible. The sound of his heart thudding loudly in his ears, and a lopsided grin on his face. Each time he would be convinced that he'd found the perfect spot, but unwittingly leaving part of his headdress poking out led to his untimely capture.

If he had the power to turn back the clock to those times, he would do it in a heartbeat. Those silly inconsequential days of masquerading as Butch Cassidy and Sitting Bull were where everything good was kept, safe and secure. Unlike now.

The day that Jacob had been hit and killed by a speeding car, was the day that changed Will's world forever. Nothing and no-one could reach him, and although his life went on to Will it felt like it only went on around him. He slowly became an observer, a ghost in his own life.

Overnight he lost all interest in the things that previously made him who he was. He stopped interacting with the people around him, and the only laughter in his life was the tinned variety which came from his mother's moronic TV sitcoms.

One by one his friends slowly drifted away. At twelve years old none of them were equipped with the patience or compassion to warrant staying close to a boy who was no longer fun, and no longer the person they knew; or wanted to get to know. He was now the outcast, the weirdo who insisted on wearing his dead brother's cowboy hat to school.

The only people that didn't avoid him were the bullies, of course. Those bastards would actively seek him out and torture him for their own entertainment.

'Wassamatta Brokeback?' they'd taunt as they ran off with Jacob's hat, ready to fling it on the school roof yet again. It would have been awful for a boy who was still capable of feeling anything.

His parents had seemed to follow some kind of a storybook cliche of failing marriage and failing at caring for their remaining son. Will guessed he'd never been their favourite, never been their priority, and without the glue of Jacob holding the three of them together still, they no longer had anything in common anymore. They had tried, in their own way, but grief had swallowed them up and left no room for anything else.

The world around Will had changed from one that had previously had its doors flung wide to welcome possibility. It felt now as though those doors were firmly closed to contain him in the metaphorical dark room that he inhabited. The only light came from its tiny spy hole that allowed him to peek out with a distorted view of the outside world.

The razor blades had helped a little. They allowed the cracks of light and tiny glimmers of calm into his world as they bit into his skin like a thousand tiny arrows. While they relieved the pressure that built behind his skin, it meant that the scars were legion. A latticework of raised tributes along his thighs and arms. Will didn't mind the way they looked too much though, and in some respects he was even proud of them, as they were all in honour of Jacob.

It wasn't enough though anymore. He needed something that would stop the numbness. Like a junkie who has to up his dose to get the same hit, he needed more than those tiny little blades to release him from the snapping jaws of the black dog.

When he came across the 3D printer on the internet, his parents had bought it for him without question. He knew they would as it was the only way they could assuage their guilt by buying him whatever he wanted; or whatever they thought he wanted.

Most of the gifts they'd bought were often duplicated by each other and then left unopened. Trainers still clean and new in their boxes, and the computer games piled under a layer of dust on the windowsill; but the printer was different. It sat on his desk surrounded by the various items that he'd made with it, each one more complex than the last. His parents had congratulated themselves that finally something had seemed to catch Will's interest.

He'd started with simple tool handles, then a pin-hole camera, followed by several kinetic sculptures which boasted unbelievably intricate workings. The technicality and the precision were so immersive on occasion that he came close to finding a kind of peace in what he was doing. If he'd been a different boy, one whose world hadn't already fallen apart, he knew that this would have been his passion.

For now, Will was just pleased that he had all the relevant parts made and ready for his new project. All he had to do was put it together and he could then bring it in for today's presentation.

School had been something to be endured over the last few years, and he had only done the bare minimum to scrape through. He had been flunking badly without really caring… until now. Now he had something to care about.

Following the itemised instructions taken from the internet, Will carefully assembled his latest piece before sitting back in his desk chair to admire his work. It amazed him he'd been able to do it. Amazed that it had been so simple. Amazed that he had finally found something that was going to stop him from hurting.

The radio was still playing some inane crap as he packed his frayed canvas school bag with everything that he needed for his presentation. Not that much as it turned out. Just his brother's hat, the pre-sourced bullets and the 3D printed gun. That was it.

Today he was finally going to be the cowboy.

I'LL NEVER FORGET
(Working on a Saturday)

BY LEWIS COOPER

"Are you happy?" she asked;
pausing the film to look at me.
It sounded more like an intended
accusation I think, but I nodded gently
and contemplated my response
to three seconds...

"I MEAN, AS A CONCEPT AND ON PAPER, I don't think many people would watch it," I admitted, "but I think I am actually enjoying it. I wouldn't say I'm happy about it but I'm entertained."

"Not with the bloody film, you idiot. With us. Are you happy with us?"

I knew exactly what she meant first time of asking but I continued to feign stupidity and ignorance with a blank, 'whadda ya mean', stare. Also, I'm well aware of my own limitations. She is the person who will only settle for a concise and rather exhaustive list of detailed romantic notions why I am indeed still over the moon she agreed to marry me.

However, I'm really not that in-the-moment, top-of-the- head, roll-off-the-tongue, kind of guy. You'd think I might have memorised some key attributes or events that I could just regurgitate in order to 'keep her sweet' but, alas, I'm not that kind of guy either.

"Do you feel like we've lost more along the way than we've actually gained?" She continued, "we're happily married, have children, a beautiful home and our health but where next. We're 34 and I don't know what comes next. Don't say 35," She knows me too well. "I know everything about you. So where do we go from there? Have we lost the romance; the excitement; that adventure?"

"We have the memories of everything we've achieved. That's romantic." I said rather matter-of-factly. I stopped short of pleading. "We have the future memories of everything we'll create. That's exciting. And we have us. That's an adventure in itself." She looked somewhat close to being convinced.

"Plus," I added, "you don't know everything about me. That would be weird."

"I'm pretty sure I do." She said threateningly, "But OK. Tell me something romantic about you that I don't know."

She glared at me. Waiting for my next move. Then whilst we sat there, playing a very perverse game of relationship chess, I saw in her eyes a longing to be loved and behind that I glimpsed everything I'll ever need.

"Alright," I agreed,

It was a Saturday, and I had to work;

I remember because you were at home, and the train was a lonely place to be.

It was early June, and the sun was shining;

I know this because you were going out that day to buy my birthday present. You don't know this.

But, after all the clues and hints, I was convinced you were buying me a table tennis table for the spare room. I was sure of it.

I was so certain of it.

I had a feeling of such secure confidence in my deciphering of the evidence that for a short while I remember thinking "This must be exactly what Poirot feels like, right before his big reveal."

I'd make a terrible detective.

I know this because goldfish do not bounce

Even half as well as ping-pong balls.

I don't remember leaving for work,

I don't remember swiping my annual train ticket on the gate.

I don't remember catching the train;

In that respect, it was like any other day.

Wake commute; work, commute; home.

Wake commute; work, commute; home.

The next thing I do remember is my phone ringing.

As the train pulled into Marylebone. And it was you.

I remember my heart racing. At just the sight of your name.

It still does, but never to the extent that I remember the feeling

Ten years later.

I was still on the train, but mid-disembarkation.

I know this because I had to steady myself by grabbing hold of a seat.

Not due to the jolt of the train, but the words that you spoke, sending a jolt through my brain.

I've never fainted in my life, but that's the closest I've ever been.

"I think you need to come home," you murmured.

I could hear it in your voice. I could hear it in your tears.

"Why?' I asked. I knew why.

I don't know why I asked.

And then after a split-second pause, that left a ringing in my ears, you said "Because I'm pregnant."

I still remember your voice. A heady conflicting mix of utter fear and happiness, unparalleled panic and excitement.

Uncertain of how I would react, with a hint of loneliness covering it all.

But there were two of you on the other end of the line now.

Little did you know that you would never be alone again!

"I'll be right there." I assured you,

"I'll be right on the next train." I said hopefully.

"I promise everything will be alright." I was guessing now.

I went and got a coffee, then headed straight to the smoking area. The next train was 12 minutes.

I smoked 3 and half cigarettes. I know this because as I lit the fourth one, it was in that moment, I realised that I had to quit.

I'd only been a dad for ten minutes.

But already I was made responsible for lifestyle changes for this baby. This was going to be a breeze!

I don't remember the train journey home, but I'm sure it was the longest forty-five minutes of my life. I know this because, well, how the hell could it not have been.

The next thing I remember is the wind in my hair and the sun on my back as I legged it down the hill into town. I remember because you'd asked me to stop at Boots pharmacy on the high street and pick up one of every pregnancy test.

"Just to be sure. Just be absolutely sure."

With the Boots plastic bag gripped tightly in my hand, I hot-footed it down the London Road, eastward out of town, past the Rising Sun.

And a waft of leftover sweet and sour pork balls; past the rows of letting agents, past your office and then the Rye. Where, out of the corner of my eye, I glimpsed the play area

Now filling up with my future; then back to our flat above the dentists.

I raced up the three flights of stairs, through the front door, and there you were, waiting, in all your pregnant glory.

Little frame and teary-eyed.

I never loved you more. We hugged.

We laughed.

I didn't cry.

But I'm sure you wanted me too. "Everything will be alright." I promised. You peed on stick after stick after stick. It was tick after tick after tick.

It still didn't seem real.

"Everything will be alright." I repeated.

I didn't know this. I remember because nobody ever knows for sure if it actually will be alright.

It was a Saturday, and I had to work;

I remember because you were at home and the train was the last place I wanted to be. It was early June and the sun was shining.

I know this because

That was a day I will never forget."

She stared at me and said nothing. I noticed her breathing had quickened. A contented, gentle smile spread slowly across her face. She leaned in and kissed me on the lips. Then she settled back into my body and pressed play on the film.

It was an avalanche that
finally halted Adam's journey.
He'd already faced a disastrous string
of setbacks, but through gritted teeth,
daring and luck, he'd overcome them all.

But gritted teeth and daring would not
open up a road buried under half a
mountain of snow. His luck had run out...

TerrorS
iNCONCeiVaBLe

BY NICK MANCE

"Y'SHOULD STAY FOR WINTER," advised the landlady of the Sky Hearth, where he'd taken lodgings for the night. "It'll all melt in its time and y'can be on y'way."

Adam took a sip of his watery mead. "When will it thaw, do you think?"

"A month or two, I should reckon."

Adam felt the slackness of his moneybag glumly.

With his progress so completely hindered, there was little left to do other than relax. After weeks of relentless movement, he finally took in the scenery.

Weycleft was a neat little town, perched upon a mountain ledge, overlooking a dense forest. Brightly painted wooden houses climbed the rocky slopes, linked by washing lines and bunting and coloured lanterns. The locals seemed friendly enough, Adam decided. The sort who might be generous when his money eventually dried up.

The town seemed as normal as any other, but for a single oddity. At the rear of the town, where the mountain formed an unscalable wall, there was an iron doorway set into the rock. An arch of illegible charcoal markings surrounded it. A semi-circle of lanterns formed its doorstep. Nobody seemed to go in or out or acknowledge the door at all.

That evening Adam dined on the cheapest platter available and fell into conversation with the local blacksmith. When Adam mentioned the door, the blacksmith's face became grave. "You don't want to know."

"Why not?"

Before the blacksmith could answer, the door of the inn opened and a dashing young man walked in. He was draped in fine furs with a plumed hat, a glamorous woman on each arm. The atmosphere in the inn changed immediately. The previously drab little bard in the corner leapt atop his stool and began playing with gusto. A score of men called out for the newcomer to join them, contending to be the first to order him an ale from the bar.

"He seems popular," said Adam.

"He's every right to be!" Said the blacksmith and promptly abandoned Adam to join the newcomer.

From the moment the man in furs entered to the point of his departure, the entire inn revolved around him. He ate and drank for free and told jokes amusing to all. When he left, half the patrons left with him.

Adam had watched the whole thing bemusedly. "What was all that about?" he asked the landlady as she picked discarded tankards off the floor.

"That's Drake," she told him. "Our protector." "What does he protect you from?"

She scoffed. "Foreigners wouldn't understand!"

Adam's coin lasted a week. The landlady was merciful and moved him to a bedroll in the cellar, assigning him the role of pot-wash and handyman.

As his face became a familiar sight around the Sky Hearth, the locals began to open up.

"Once a year, every year," recounted an old man, as Adam slowly wiped his table.

"Our Drake goes through that door to face terrors inconceivable. He goes in, he comes out, and then we're safe for another year."

"Safe from what?"

"From terrors inconceivable, like I said."

"What sort of terrors?"

But he was told off for asking stupid questions.

Drake was only an occasional patron of the Sky Hearth. Adam saw snatches of him around town, usually followed by a trail of admirers, but the moments were rare.

"He spends most of his time in that mansion of his," the landlady told him. "Preparing himself for the next time he needs to go through the door."

Adam had seen the house from afar–balconies and turrets, surrounded by a walled garden, perched high on a ridge overlooking the rest of town.

"He's wealthy then?"

"Wealthy!" the landlady scoffed. "He doesn't need money! We built him that house."

"Just because he goes through a door once a year?"

"Because he faces terrors inconceivable! To protect us! I told you foreigners wouldn't understand."

The longer Adam stayed in Weycleft, the more curious about Drake and the door he became. Nobody could give him a solid answer about what sort of terrors lay beyond the door. They were happy not knowing. Happy that only Drake knew.

Choosing a day when the landlady was in a good mood, he dared to challenge her. "How do you know he's telling the truth? None of you have ever seen these inconceivable terrors. Perhaps there's nothing on the other side."

She smiled at him as though he were a child. "Y'should see him when he comes out. He's pale and shaking and mute for a week afterwards, cos of the horrors he's seen."

That gave Adam thought, but his reason won out. Such symptoms were easy to fake. Was it all a charade? Drake had the entire town under his thumb, and all it seemed to cost him was a week's pantomime each year.

As winter thawed to spring, Adam was informed that the mountain road was passable again. He stayed. The day of the door was drawing close and Adam wanted to see it for himself. His journey could wait.

A sombre mood had settled over the town. The musicians had retired their instruments. The bunting disappeared. Drake had become a recluse in his mansion.

The day of the door began with an ominous gong, signalling the start of a fast. Nobody appeared in the streets all day. Adam waited in the cellar, hungry and bored, yet intrigued by the thought of what was to come.

The landlady came for him in the evening. "Put this on," she instructed, presenting him with a large, black cloak. Adam wrapped himself in it and accepted a long candle. Then they joined a stream of townsfolk drifting sombrely towards the cliff wall and the door to the mountain. Drake was there, at the centre of a growing crowd. He was dressed in elaborate robes, his skin marked with charcoal runes. His face was set towards the door, his eyes wide and staring, chest heaving.

Adam's scepticism wavered. The atmosphere of dread made it hard to be cynical. It felt like something altogether otherworldly was about to happen. He looked at all the faces glowing in candlelight. They fixed their scared eyes upon Drake.

The sun sank lower in the sky until it was lost behind the mountains. A mighty hush fell.

Drake slowly looked around at them all, taking in each face one at a time. Then he turned, dragged open the door and entered.

As one, the townsfolk dropped to their knees. Adam's landlady grabbed his arm and pulled him down. "Now we pray," she said.

"Who are we praying to?"

But she was already mumbling incoherently with her face to the ground.

Adam looked around at them all and listened to the subdued babbling of their prayers. He looked at the door and suddenly all his doubts returned. Drake was playing them for fools!

He stood and walked forwards. A few people looked up and hissed at him, but he pressed on. There was gasp as he stepped past the circle of lanterns and continued to the door.

"Stop him!" someone called out in a harsh whisper, but none of them moved.

Adam paused at the door. A last moment of doubt. Then he pulled it open and stepped into the mountain.

The door closed.

The townsfolk returned to their prayers with greater fervour. At midnight they broke their fast and then some of them slept, while others continued to pray. They took it in turns, right the way through the night.

As the first rays of a new day rose along the mountain wall, the aroused sleepers and the townsfolk watched the door expectantly.

After a while there was a grinding creak, and it swung open. For a moment there was only darkness. Then a pale figure staggered out. It came stumbling to the edge of the lanterns and fell to the ground. The crowd surged forwards, swamping the shaking form. The landlady fought her way to the front.

"What happened?" she asked. "Where's Drake?"

Trembling, Adam raised his eyes to hers. "We're safe," he croaked. "Safe for another year!"

The End of Innocence

BY ELSIE LEIPER

It had been the hottest
summer in decades.
Lawns had dried up, ice
creams had sold out, and
the public swimming
pool had been packed
for weeks.

THE WEATHER WAS SO HOT THAT DOING any form of work became unbearable, and so the days were spent sunbathing and gorging on ice lollies. Being kids, we'd had no problem with this... The adults, too exhausted from the heat to protest when we asked to go out, and so we had total freedom.

At the beginning of the holidays we'd enjoyed walking into town. A new shopping centre had recently been built, which included an arcade. We loved nothing more than pouring piles of shiny pennies into those machines, on the off chance that we might win a stuffed teddy or a bar of chocolate. Until the third week of the summer holidays we had been unsuccessful and my younger brother, George, was getting fed up.

"These machines are rigged", he complained, after losing his third game of pinball.

"They're not rigged", my sister, Esme, argued, "You're just bad at it."

"I'm bored with the arcade, anyway. Can't we go get an ice cream?"

"I don't have any money for an ice cream. You wasted the last on that stupid pinball game", I retorted.

He held up a grubby coin, "I still have a pound left."

"That won't be enough. Let's just go home. Dinner will be ready soon, anyway." I headed towards the door, Esme trailing behind me, but George stayed put. "Hurry up, George."

He glanced over at me, slotting his last pound into the machine.

"Fine, waste your money. See if I care."

This only seemed to spur him on. Tongue hanging out in concentration, he expertly pulled the silver levers. The machine's lights flashed wildly as the ball bounced around the metal cage. I folded my arms, patiently waiting for the game to end, but it didn't. The now sweaty George was still managing to keep the ball moving. Esme watched intensely over his shoulder, her enormous eyes even wider. Finally, the screen flashed: NEW HIGH SCORE!

"Yes!", George yelled, his arms raised in victory.

The machine whirred, and a trail of orange tokens appeared from one of its slots. George grabbed them greedily, running over to the arcade's shop. Stuffed animals, lollipops, bouncy balls and plastic jewellery lined the walls of the shop in a colourful confusion. Luckily George, who had been surveying the prizes for weeks, knew exactly what he wanted.

Smiling brightly, he handed the cashier his token, "Can I have the binoculars, please?"

He marvelled at them as we walked out of the arcade. The cheaply made binoculars with garish red plastic trim, and already scratched lenses, but yet he seemed to think they were worth a million pounds.

"Everything looks tiny!", he giggled.

I sighed, "You have them the wrong way round, George."

He ignored me, continuing to laugh at the tiny cars the entire journey home.

The next morning was eerily quiet. My parents, hungover from the night before, had asked me to take George and Esme out for some peace. Since it was early, town wasn't an option, so we walked to the moor. I was in a terrible mood after I'd been rudely awaken by a bored Esme in the early hours of the morning. It didn't help that the heatwave had made the nights unbearably hot, and even with the fan turned on, I struggled to sleep.

As soon as I reached the moor, I regretted my decision. There was a powerful stench of cow dung and rotting plants, which the heat only intensified.

"It smells, Emmy. Can't we go somewhere else?", Esme protested.

She had a point, but I was still irritated, so I refused.

"No. You wanted to go out, so we're going here."

George, who was fascinated by creepy-crawlies and all things disgusting, didn't mind. He held his tiny, plastic binoculars to his face, spying on the ants.

"Do you think there will be any toads in the river?", he asked, making Esme squeal in disgust.

"How should I know?", I replied coldly.

I hopped over the wooden fence guarding the river, Esme and George following close behind. Crayfish crawled amongst the rocks and mud that lined the river bed, which immediately captured their attention. Eager for a moment alone, I wandered upstream. Here the water was grossly covered by pennywort, flax and miscellaneous weeds. Amid the rushes a small frog balanced precariously on a lily pad, it's eyes wide and darting. I was about to call George over when I noticed a child's shoe bobbing up and down beside it.

Before I could fish it out I heard George shout, "Emmy! There's something in the weeds!"

I rushed over to them. He had his binoculars to his face again and was pointing towards the other side of the river.

"Emmy, there's something in weeds", he repeated.

"It's probably just a frog, George. I just saw one."

"It's not a frog, Emmy. I think it's a monster."

I rolled my eyes.

"Fine! If you don't believe me, see for yourself."

He handed me his binoculars. Despite having only just been won from the arcade, they were surprisingly effective. I could see the weeds much better now, and I realised George was right. There was something in the water.

"Can you see it?", he asked nervously.

"I can see something."

"I knew it!", Esme cried, "There's a monster in the river"

"Don't be silly. Look, if it will make you feel better I'll go see what's there."

Esme looked up at me with gigantic eyes, "Would you?"

The water was much colder and deeper than I expected. Slowly, I waded towards the reeds; the stones cutting into my feet. On land, George and Esme cheered on.

"Be careful, Emmy!", they warned.

I smiled back at them, snatching a stick that was stuck in the river's current. Cautiously, I used the stick to prod the weeds aside. They parted like a curtain, revealing a horrific sight. A pale, lifeless face stared back at me. It was hard to tell how long she'd been dead. Her body was bloated from the water, and the little creatures that inhabited the weeds had eaten away at it. Stunned, I dropped the stick, allowing the reeds to snap back in place.

"What is it?", Emmy squealed.

I paused for a moment, trying to catch my breath. "Nothing", I stuttered, "Just a frog."

I thought my flimsy lie had concealed the horrific truth, but poor George had seen the corpse through the lenses of his binoculars. That night as I lay in my bed, listening to the hum of my fan and the chirps of the crickets, I heard him cry out.

"There's a monster in the river! Mummy, there's a monster!."

Two sets of footsteps padded across the landing, and I hushed George back to sleep. "There are no such things as monsters, darling", my mum whispered, "You're safe here with me."

His cries eventually subsided, and the house was silent again. But I still couldn't sleep. The same phrase repeated continually in my mind. There are no such things as monsters, there are no such things as monsters. The words tossed and turned around my brain like clothes in a washing machine, and the more I repeated it the more I doubted it. Monsters didn't have fangs or claws. They didn't lurk under beds and in rivers. But they were real. They lived amongst us, undetected, but harbouring a darkness within them. A darkness that could drive someone to kill a person. They were more dangerous than the monsters I had read about in fairytales because they were imperceptible. They walked among us and one was right under our noses.

This thought hovered in the air for the rest of the summer, like mosquitoes over water. I locked doors after 9pm, new curfews were set for children, and we left the once bustling streets of the town deserted after dusk.

The summer holidays couldn't end soon enough, and I was grateful to have school again to take my mind off of things. The heatwave eventually ended, and with it left the thoughts of the girl in the river. I had almost forgotten it entirely until a rainy day in October. I was decorating the garden for Halloween when I spotted something buried beneath the dirt. Using my hands, I pushed the mud away, uncovering a familiar object. George's binoculars. For a moment I thought about washing them up, and giving them to him as a gift, but I quickly decided against it. I knew very well why he had discarded them, and the last thing I wanted was for the memories of that summer to return. Better to leave things buried in the past.

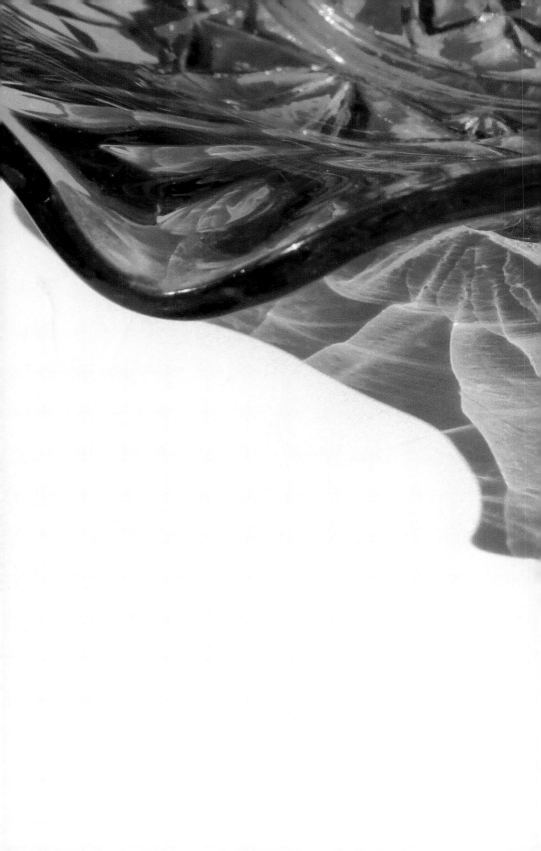

A DIVALI TALE

BY BARBARA PEARMAN

"Tomorrow I will show you something you will
never forget," he had promised, as they parted at
the end of another memorable day...

Rayansh has been her guide for three weeks, on an incredible journey from one Indian city to another. His expert knowledge and attention to every detail, designed to make her dream holiday a reality, has been more than she could have hoped for. It seems impossible that anything can outdo The Taj Mahal, the Amber Fort, the teeming humanity in the streets of Old Delhi and the magical train ride to Amritsar at the foot of the Himalayas.

But here they are at The Golden Temple. And it is incredible. A million diamonds shimmering on a lapis blue lake, with the temple, a nugget of shining gold, at its heart. The surrounding buildings so white glow, translucent, in the sun's glare. Women in saris fill the space with colour. Pure, like the paint squeezed fresh on an artist's palette. Or a rainbow, fallen from the sky.

She waits, impatient to see Rayansh again. His name means 'Ray of Light' and this is how she thinks of him now. It is hot, so she sits, arranges her pretty cotton skirt round her pale bare legs to protect them from the sun, pulls a canvas hat from her brightly coloured woven bag, covers her head and dons a chic pair of sunglasses. She is happy to spend time soaking up the atmosphere. Reminiscing about the wonderful days and nights they have spent exploring and getting to know each other. The Temple is, for Angelisa the highlight. Being in this space she has dreamed about visiting for so long is both gratifying and disappointing.

It is the last of their destinations. Every dream must end and soon she will be going home.

Her thoughts constantly return to Rayansh. She had been warned about the charms of Indian men but as soon as they met she felt a connection never experienced before. His inner calm and gentle manner so unlike the brash egotistical men at home. Overtly masculine, his angular jaw contrasts perfectly with the sensuality of his full mouth. A face, handsome without conceit. His quiet assured confidence; the relaxed way he walks; the way his strong manicured hands rake through his hair when he is concentrating. She loves all these things about him.

He arrives. She is momentarily astonished by his appearance. "Why have you shaved your head?

He hesitates. Stays silent for a while, then gazing past her.

It's just a temporary thing, I think. Come, let us eat before we start our visit.

Rayansh leads her to a small, intimate restaurant. They talk, comfortable in each other's company and oblivious to those around them. Her hands are expressive, her voice full of wonder for the places he has shown her. He listens attentively, occasionally touching his head as if confirming the absence of his thick dark hair. Her animated expressions fascinate him. He can't take his eyes from hers. They glow like amber jewels lit by the light inside her. Her blond curls bob about as she enthuses and exclaims, darting from one subject to another. They cannot see it yet, but they have become soul mates. Rayansh guides her through the temple grounds. Crystalline marble floors glow underfoot. Their eyes squint with the intensity of its reflected light.

They visit the dark smoky kitchens. As they enter the Langar, their eyes struggle to adjust to the change in light. High ceilings, grey concrete walls and stone floors give the building an industrial feel. Men, women and children sit cross-legged on the floor to receive their meal. The air is filled with a million specs of dust, like tiny fireflies. Steam rises and takes the pungent smell of spices on its journey, by way of a shaft of light, to the open roof and out into the wider world.

A cacophony of noise from voices, kitchen machinery and music assaults their ears. Volunteers and visitors alike are barefoot and the shuffling of feet ebbs and flows, like waves on a beach, as they come and go.

Hundreds work to keep up with the enormous task. With each onion chopped or roti flattened you can hear them chant 'wahe guru..wahe guru' invoking the name of God. They join in. Huge iron pots containing hundreds of kilos of dhal, rice and vegetable curry simmer away, stirred with ladles the size of rowing oars. The pungent smell of cumin, ginger, chilli and coriander pervade the steamy air. Metal serving plates, in a conveyor belt of washing up, clank and crash like a thousand cymbals.

The Temple has surpassed her expectations. His time as her guide is over and they are both reluctant to say goodbye. Rayansh hands her a piece of paper.

'Tonight is a special time for me. You will find me here. I hope you will come. Your presence will help me decide.'

As night falls, she makes her way through the dark narrow alleyways outside the temple grounds. Windows lit by a thousand lights cast flickering shadows on those passing by. The hypnotic sound of singing bowls draws her near to a small temple. Deep voiced chanting comes from within.

Her eyes adjust to the light as she enters. A stone Buddha dominates the space, lit by hundreds of flickering candles, his features carved sharply by the shadows. A dozen young monks sit cross-legged in a circle. Their saffron and orange robes glow in the candlelight. Their skin looks silken. Their expressions are passive. Content.

It is a scene of calm serenity, but she feels unsettled. One of the men turns and their eyes meet. It is Rayansh. Clasping her hands over her face in despair, she cries. *'What a fool I am.'* She stumbles back into the black night and runs, tears flooding her eyes back to the Temple.

The water around the Temple has become silver foil in the moonlight. Reflections of the fireworks, like giant drops of coloured ink, spread over its surface. It is a display, both above and below, like no other she has ever seen.

The sky returns to its starry self. A shooting star momentarily marks it like a silver pen. The buildings sleep beneath their dark cloak of night. The crowd disperses. She is alone. The temple grounds have fallen silent. It is time to leave.

Deep in her troubled thoughts, she is unaware that a familiar figure stands before her.

He calls to her, "Angelisa."

Dressed once again in his denim jeans and black t-shirt, his saffron robe is draped across his shoulder. He moves forward and takes her hands in his. The robe slips to the floor. He has no further use for it.

A SENSE OF PLACE

by Brian Munnery

The rhythmic pounding of my feet forced me on, despite the sweat stinging my eyes, till I reached the dune's summit.

I didn't stop, but the glimpse of the verdant valley and foot hills of the Kavinia mountains beyond gave me heart and I steadied my pace for the muscle aching descent...

THE FIRST SCATTERING OF TREES BROUGHT a welcome relief from the Grecian sun, the cool of the forest allowing me to think. The Kyrinos International Marathon had been a staggered start and, while I had passed quite a few runners, I was uncertain of my position. It didn't help either that some route stewards weren't on station and for the last five miles or so I'd seen no sign of them nor, and this was worrying, no route markers either. The long climbing stretch of the Kyrinos plains was practically a desert and running through the forest fringe centred my thoughts.

Had I missed the route? The track I was on wasn't that well trod either but I still pressed on. It was only the undergrowth closing in on either side of the path which convinced me I was lost. I slowed to a walk, hoping against hope but a momentary flash of white ahead set me running again. Whoever, of whatever it was, had vanished when I burst into the sunlit clearing. I realised then that the race of a lifetime had turned into just that, but not in the way I'd intended.

Even if I could retrace my steps, any chance of a finish position would be lost and my time, embarrassing, so I slowed to a brisk walk which, after an hour of sylvan solitude, changed to an enjoyable casual stroll.

So much so, I hadn't realised the overhead canopy was thinning and with it returned the oppressive heat of a Grecian afternoon. The valley was widening, small meadows breaking up the trees and, judging by the grazing sheep, there must be a habitation of some sorts and I was right. Rounding an outcrop of a sheer cliff face revealed some fifty dwellings clustered around a white adobe church, its green, onion-like, spire dominating the crowding houses.

Desultory barking heralded my presence, raising the heads of those working in the fields and around the houses. I caught the flutter of murmured interest and people drifted to line the single track leading into the village.

With my very limited Greek, I smiled, 'ya-su-ing' to my left and right, men and women alike smiling back, seeming to understand me, but I couldn't comprehend their greetings. The growing crowd forced me to a stop outside the church and I was at a loss to explain myself, for you can only repeat 'ya-su' or 'ya-sas' for a few times; any longer and you become a gormless, grinning idiot.

Exasperated, I declared in English, "Sorry, I am English, Ingesee? – and cannot speak Greek." After all, I was only here to run that bloody marathon!

"Greetings my son. Be at peace and welcome to Avonsia." The greeting, in excellent English, came from a rotund, beaming man, waddling through the throng. Judging by his brown cassock, I assumed he was a local priest.

Which was what he proved to be: Father Beri, the village priest, to whom I related my woes. He, in turn, translated to the villagers who murmured their appreciation when he mentioned 'Marathon'. The villagers pointed fingers at my running gear, murmuring their understanding. What followed next seemed to be an impromptu decision by the villager to organise a fete in my honour, encouraged by Father Beni who, I suspected, had an un-used Saint for just such an occasion.

On his instructions they ushered me to the village bathhouse – men's section – where a roof top stone cistern, fed by a mountain stream, drenched me in lukewarm water which, all too soon, became a freezing cold shower, hastening my exit.

Washed and dried, it provided me with an oversized white shirt and voluminous trousers while they whisked away my running gear to be laundered, I retained my shoes. Back in the shady square, they guided me to a seat next to Father Beri, at the head of a number of trestle tables formed into a square which the womenfolk were loading with food and wine. All that, plus jaunty tunes from a whirling accordion, set the seal on a brilliant day and night.

That festivities ended somewhere around midnight,   Father Beri appointed Maria to lead me, with her smiling beauty, through the festivities and the Greek language—to a straw-filled mattress in a lean-to shack. Covering me with a blanket, smelling strongly of horses, she planted a gentle kiss and left me to a sleep with dreams such as I had never had before—Nirvana!

Too soon though, I awoke to a cock crowing with Father Beri gently shaking me to accept a strong black coffee. In a daze, I dressed and staggered out into the deserted square where, already mounted, Father Beri, handed me the reins of downcast looking mule, ignoring my protests at never having ridden before. Somehow, though, I found myself as despondent as the mule, trailing after Father Beri and down the mountainside.

An hour's riding brought us to a river, the track leading through a ford, the other side of which Father Brown bid me dismount. "Another seven miles" nodding towards the horizon "and you'll find the road to Kyrinos and possibly passage with a passing cart but here, Michael, is where we part. May the Good Lord protect you."

With a last smile, he tied the reins of my mount to his and rode back over the ford. I watched them briefly before turning to look at what lay before me. As far as the eye could see was the typical coastal prairie with no signs of life or habitation, and when I looked back again Father Beri had vanished into the mists which cloaked the foothills of the Kavinia mountains.

My seven mile trudge ended when I reached a crest overlooking the coast and–oh joy! A two lane dual modern highway stretched before me, not the country road implied by Father Beri and – with a bus stop!

A half hour wait, plus a two-hour, four-euro journey [I do keep a couple of Euro notes with me] found me outside the Kyrinos Mecure Hotel. "Key please to 209."

The receptionist looked blankly at me. "Sorry sir. Do you have a reservation?" I smiled, explaining I'd been staying here for the last seven days, part of the UK's marathon entrants. Her wide-eyed expression should have warned me, but I pressed on. "I'm Michael Brown, occupying room 209" and stabbed a finger at the Room Occupancy list. Giving a weak smile, she picked up the phone. The smart suited man who appeared proved to be the manager. His expression, following the receptionist's explanation, alarmed me–his face went white!

"You must me mistaken, sir. The Marathon was run nearly two years ago and, yes, a Michael Brown, English and a participant in the race did stay here. He disappeared whilst competing and was never seen again. Despite days of intensive searching, we found no trace of him. It was assumed he'd fallen, died and had been eaten by the wolves or boars that roam these parts".

He was staring wildly at me, and I turned to catch my reflection in a mirror. I didn't recognise the wild-haired, bearded ruffian staring back at me. The white clothing of yesterday was brown, stained and tattered, the results of months of wear. I could understand his disbelief.

In dumb reply, I emptied my bag of running gear, complete with the start number, onto the desk. In the stunned silence that followed, I gratefully sipped the glass of Ouzo the receptionist offered while the manager babbled excitedly into the phone.

SAY WHAT?

BY JACK STEVENS

His name was Fletch. Actually,
we'd christened him Norman
Stanley Fletcher; you know, after
Ronnie Barker's character in
Porridge, but we called him
Fletch...

WE THOUGHT IT WAS FUNNY because it sounded like 'fetch'. He wasn't a recognised breed or anything, and he certainly would not win any beauty competitions. He was just an ordinary dog. A non-descript grey colour with off-white bits, and a kind of vacant expression, a mongrel. A Heinz 57, my dad would have called him.

He was smooth in places and wiry in others and a bit straggly across the shoulder, like he was wearing a scarf he'd borrowed from another dog, got used to and forgotten to give back. He moved kind of diagonally when he chased something; like how a cut-and- shut car never runs true. His back end looking like it was in danger of overtaking his front section which travelled that bit slower.

But he was ours, and we just went with it, like families do. It wasn't like we were the Famous Five or anything, but he was always involved, sort of on the edges of everything. A spectator, with his watchful, droopy eyes, tongue lolling out of his mouth, looking for all the world like he was smiling.

You're probably expecting me to say how we all loved him desperately, despite a rocky start type stuff. He chewed an expensive pair of my wife's boots, ate a signed Sea Sick Steve CD and we were considering giving him up. But then he redeemed himself by pulling a toddler out of a well? With maybe a group family shot of us all on the front of The Evening Post grinning like idiots with the 'hero dog' up front and centre?

Well, I'm sorry, but it wasn't like that at all; he just sorted of fitted in as part of the picture and we all existed around each other. No big deal, just our little family group, in our little family world, in our little family way. We walked him and we fed him. The kids grew up, and we all got that bit older, with him ageing seven years to each one of ours.

Then one day, we had teenage children who always had somewhere else to be and an old dog who didn't.

The boys were doing their own thing; disappearing with ugly, hormone-faced, youths for hours on end before returning to grunt something and then sleep for twelve hours after their exhausting day, presumably pressing x or circle. My wife and I went to work, came home and did the things people do on any day in a suburban close on a housing estate in South Gloucestershire.

Fletch had not been himself for a while, and I suspected we were coming to the end of the road. Don't get me wrong, it was sad and everything, but, like I say, he was only a dog. At the end I didn't see it coming... except I did and I didn't want to, so I pretended I didn't. He just kind of slowed up, wound down. His legs stiffened and grey sprouted around his soft muzzle. His eyes took on that slightly far-away look that you see in old people preoccupied with a different life, remembered in black and white where children looked like angry mini adults in itchy suits and haircuts. I wondered if he had his own sepia snap shots stored away of whatever constitutes precious memories for a family pet.

I'd taken to letting him sleep on the bed with us. Not because I'm David Attenborough or anything; more because if he was going to have a crafty pee in the night, I'd like to know about it and let him out into the back garden. He was pretty good to be fair, and I was usually up in the night anyway with my aging bladder.

The morning it happened, I woke in that limbo land when you do not understand what day it is or what time it is; Sunday and nearly lunchtime? Or oh no, it's Tuesday and you're late for work. I'd spent the last few days decorating the kitchen, and every sinew ached even before I opened my eyes.

Yesterday on hands and knees, I'd been filling the claw-scraped crevices Fletch had made in the plaster by the back door, part of the fingerprint we'd left on the house as a family, like the horizontal pen marks on the kitchen door-jam showing the heights of the kids as they'd grown.

I surfaced and there he was, a foot away, spread out like a human head on the pillow, staring earnestly into my face. His nostrils twitched as he smelled the awake inside me. I closed my eyes again, voice croaky with lack of use through the night, I said,

"Hello, old fella. How're you doing?"

The answer appeared to originate from an area just outside my head, a halo of sound some inches from my skull. Like wireless headphones.

"You're no spring chicken yourself these days, you know." I opened my eyes and Fletch winked one of his closed, a smile playing about the soft wrinkles of his forehead. "Ah ha, it's only taken you a lifetime but finally you're tuned in." He kind of shrugged his ears, "Well my lifetime anyway."

I tensed my shoulders to sit up.

"I wouldn't do that if I were you," the Fletch head-voice said, "The link is pretty fragile, and it'd be a shame to break it at this late juncture." I stayed where I was, deciding this was a pleasurable dream.

"Stick your tongue in Dad, makes you look simple." I recognised my catch- phrase, I'd said to him for years. He licked his lips and his own nose, wide and wet.

"Is that what your voice sounds like?" I asked him pointlessly. "You sound like David Suchet."

"15 years of non-verbal communication and that's the best you can do?" His eyes laughed. "Yeah I suppose inside your head it does. Maybe in somebody else's it might be different." He paused, "How the hell would I know?"

I looked at his familiar grizzled face,

"I'm not really sure of what to say." I said.

"Me neither. So many times I've wanted to tell you something. And now..." He pulled a face. "You OK?"

"I can't get comfortable." He said, "Worse in the mornings, but I doubt that's going to be an issue after today." I felt a thickening in my throat. Now I really didn't know what to say.

We lay in silence for a time. His breathing deepened, and I wondered if he'd fallen asleep again. I cleared my throat, and he opened his eyes.

"How do you know?"

He shrugged an ear.

"Now don't go getting all dopey about it. It's just time, that's all." I stared into his cloudy irises.

"We've had a good time though, haven't we?" I hesitated, fearing the answer to my next question. "Was I, a good master?"

"Master?" I swear to God he laughed at me. "Yeah, you wish, chubby. Who picks up after whom around here?" I laughed back at him. With him.

"Whom? Get you with your newfound grammatically correct voice." I hesitated, "So, have you enjoyed life? Were we a nice family to live with?" I suddenly remembered all the times I'd yelled at him for chewing something, the times I'd promised a walk and then decided I was too tired and it could wait until tomorrow.

He said softly, "It's alright, don't feel bad. To be honest once you've done one lap of the park you've seen all there is to see. I like scaring the crap out of the ducks, though. They're prissy little creatures." His lip twitched. "Oh, and you throw like a girl."

We lay looking at each other. I suddenly needed to do something and clambered out of bed looking for my discarded clothes.

"Come on boy, let's go for a nice gentle stroll, somewhere nice." He didn't answer, and I turned back to the bed. I knew before I knew if you know what I mean? I'd moved, and I'd broken the connection.

I stepped to the edge of the bed. His eyes were closed, and he looked peaceful, an older version of the puppy we'd once brought home. Much later, I'd wonder at my idiocy. All the things I could have asked, should have asked. The force that had been Fletch had gone and had been replaced by something more real, more vital;losing him.

I sat and stroked his bony head with my fingertips and started rehearsing how I'd break the news to the rest of Fletch's pack when they woke. They'd not so much as looked at him in weeks; they were going to be devastated.

The Dreamcatcher

BY CAROLA KOLBECK

The long, dark hall lay still, the
only sound a small humming
from the machines, each
skilfully attached to the
heads of ragged, thin,
sometimes skeletal
figures.

THE ONLY LIGHT WAS A FAINT, muddy green glint coming from the overhead fluorescent tubes, their neon shimmer eerily dipping the hall into stillness. Nothing moved, all was quiet... A small camera suddenly moved to one of the narrow stretchers. The body on it had begun to twitch and now was progressively shaking more until it was in fits and triggered a red light above its station. An alarm started, the shrill sound echoing around the now ruby red hall, loud enough to wake a corpse, but none of the other bodies moved. A small door in the far corner of the wall flew open and three figures dressed in white overalls followed a tall, thin man wearing a large laboratory coat that travelled behind him like an ill-fated cape. The small procession hurried to the offending station and one overall slapped a button which silenced the alarm. The man in the coat studied the small screen, tapped a few buttons, moved a few graphs, then threw his hands in the air.

"Useless!" His gruff voice smacked across the hall and he nodded to the first of his followers. "Terminate it. We can't get any excellent information from that. Those dreams are hideous." He turned on his heel and stormed back towards the door, the other two following him.

The remaining overall held the small screen and observed it. His head turned to the body, still twitching and jerking. He looked at the small syringe that lay ready on a tray next to the monitor. Slowly, he picked it up, holding it above the erratically moving figure. His gaze steadily on the needle, he squeezed the liquid into nothing. He discarded the small cannula and then proceeded to unplug the wires from the body's head. The twitching stopped immediately, and her eyes opened. "Not a sound", he hissed, helping her to sit.

"There, put this on", he handed her a white overall. "We must hurry. They will be back soon."

Frail limbs, dangling like a rag doll, the head too large for the emaciated body, the eyes hollow, dark and without a glint of life, the trembling figure of a young woman pulled the white garment onto her legs. Quickly, he grabbed her by one of her pointy elbows to stop her from toppling over.

"What about all the cameras?" Her voice was raspy and shaking, and her eyes darted frantically around the hall.

"I have it covered", he said grimly, zipping up her boiler suit. Like a fragile statue, he gently lent her against the stretcher and unhooked a small sack still attached to the drip. A thick, pale, grey blue liquid barely moved as he held it out to her.

"Take that", he thrusted it against her bony chest.

"What is it?" Her voice was now barely audible.

"Your dreams. All the good ones. If you ever have any chance of leading a normal life, you will need them. You'll have enough bad ones to give you nightmares for eternity," he chuckled disingenuously.

"Come, they will be after us, we don't have long!" He grabbed her ice-cold hand and pulled her up, but her legs gave way. He rummaged in his pocket and pulled out a small, silver tin that had an intricate emblem of a moon engraved on the inside of the lid. In the tin were two pills. He handed her the pink one.

"What's this?" She held it between two of her fingers, her skin so pale it seemed translucent.

"It'll give you energy to walk by yourself. The cover's blown if I have to drag you there."

"What about the green pill?"

His eyes met hers and, without blinking, he muttered: "That's a different way out."

She nodded meekly and swallowed the pill. It got stuck in her throat and she started to retch.

"We may as well...", he uttered, unscrewing a small opening of the pouch of the grey, mysterious mass. "Drink. Now!"

The goo was thick and gloopy like cake batter and it tasted bitter sweet. She struggled again, gulping and choking, but then she could feel the pill sliding down.

Immediately a warm sensation rose from her stomach and spread to her arms and legs, her chest and then to her cheeks. Suddenly, she felt able to stand without a prop. Her companion dragged her forward and she hurried towards some huge mirrored doors. He ripped a card from his pocket and held it against a sensor that blinked neon green immediately. As the doors slowly opened, like snakes gliding silently towards their prey, she glimpsed herself and gasped.

"Hurry!", he hissed and grabbed her hand again, rushing through the doors that closed shut without a sound behind them.

"Wait!" She pulled him back. "What's your name?"

He hesitated a moment and squinted.

"Elano", he said briskly. "Dreamcatcher."

"I'm..."

"I know you're Lily", he snapped and pulled her forward again.

No sooner had they reached another set of doors, alarms screeched and bleated and loud bangs of iron shutters smashing into the floor thundered, making the floor vibrate. Her eyes widened and her heart was throbbing against her ribcage.

The door in front of them jerked open as another overall reached for some keys and fiddled with them before ramming one of the keys into the lock. Elano nodded at the person in passing and started running. A shot echoed against the walls and made her ears ring. As she glanced back mid- run, the white suit was slumped on the floor, speckles of red and a trickle of blood staining the immaculate whiteness.

More shots echoed as they fled through an open side gate. She stumbled and nearly fell down some stairs, but Elano held and steadied her.

"We're nearly there. Down here!" His hand clasped over hers, her paper thin, ghostly skin, in stark contrast to his dark and warm one. They flew down the bumpy stair well, tripping over stones, crashing into the hard, damp and slimy walls. A salty, crisp and spicy breeze wrapped around them as they reached a narrow corridor, a faint orange light flickering at the end of it. Elano pushed her in front of him, shoving her along, and then threw them both into a small, wooden dinghy that rocked so hard it threatened to expel her into the dark waves that lapped against the rocks. He thrust the pouch of dreams into her arms and untangled the rope, then started the engine which stuttered to life, gently bobbing the boat up and down, jittering forward and steadily moving from the gaping hole they had escaped from. A bundle of voices, first subdued, then getting louder, travelled towards them as they both stared transfixed towards the shore, where now a huge fortress, looming over the coastline of, what Lily could to make out, a small island, dominated by a monstrosity of a castle.

"Lie down", Elano ordered, his voice brisk and brittle.

"Who are you? Why are you helping me?" Lily felt weaker by the second, the fire in her body a mere smouldering of ashes, the flames succumbed to the waves of the sea.

"You're our only hope." Machine gun shots peppered the air, and Lily cowered lower into the boat.

"I - I - ...Why'd'you call me Lily?" Her voice was a desperate pleading, confused and lost amongst the cold and cutting shots being fired.

"You're the daughter of the chief. They kidnapped you and brought you here to the dream farm. They harvest our good dreams, then sell them for a lot of money and questionable favours to the rich. What's left for us, the scum of the Metropole, are the nightmares, the hunters, the torturers, the ones that mess with your head before you wake up." He paused. "If we get you back, they'll have hope, so they'll fight." Elano pushed back his sleeve to reveal a tattoo of a moon, the same she had seen on the little tin. He fished out the trinket and opened it, grabbing the lonely capsule.

"I'm sorry you must do the last bit by yourself." The green pill disappeared in his mouth so quickly, she stopped breathing.

"I'll catch you when you're dreaming", he smiled, his teeth gleaming in the moonlight, before he flopped over to her feet. Lily swallowed a scream and tears shot into her eyes. A dim light caught her attention as the dinghy bobbed along, and she could make out the shape of a rickety fishing boat.

"Lily, wake up, wake up!" Bright eyes in a dark face stared at her.

"Not a sound", he hissed, helping her to sit. "We must hurry. They will be back soon", he mumbled as he unplugged the wires from her head.

What you wish for

BY ROB ROBSON

Brian hadn't realised that being careful to be careless would be so difficult. Clean by nature, he washed his hands repeatedly during the day – and in the last few years had even acquired some hand gel for added comfort of mind...

UNBEKNOWN TO HIM, he was referred to as the 'hand-wash guy' at work when colleagues often struggled to bring his face to mind. Sniggering snorts of laughter as the penny dropped. An anonymous number in the ranks of the giant office, hidden behind the large screen and happily invisible in the corridors and kitchen areas. Office furniture his jungle, corduroy and tweed his camouflage.

So many surfaces, so many other hands and the amount of times he had left the gents having witnessed poor sanitary practices. He was damned if he was going to add some other idiots' festering disease to his own person on top of the drudgery of having to work daily in the mind shrinking corporation. They might well already have his soul on toast, but he was fighting like hell to keep them off his body. Not that anybody there would associate him with fighting for anything. Quiet bloke in accounts, old-fashioned suit, comb over hair, sits in the corner, you know, wrings his hands a lot. The person you would least imagine you would want to become.

Then it arrived. Finally, what he had been worrying about, what he would have warned them all about had he the guts to speak louder than a whisper. Suddenly the world changed, and he was quickly ushered away from his cramp office environment. Furlough. Such an understated word for the best gift he had ever received. Go home, don't come into work and we will keep paying you. Deal, shake on it, on second thoughts, better not. Bugger the restrictions, it was like retiring early on full pay, something he would never be able to do, in normal circumstances.

Then to cap it all, Lockdown. Which meant all the other imbeciles that encroached in to his meagre life and personal space were going to be prevented from going out. No brushing up against him in the packed commuter train, no infected breath on the back of his neck as he waited on the busy platform and no marauding drunk arseholes shouting down the street in the early hours. He now knew how it felt to find a faulty ATM that kept on paying out, only that he was getting wishes rather than cash.

It was at the start of the third week at home when he decided he wasn't ever going to go back to work. It was another day before he had worked out how. Throwing caution to the wind, he walked to the supermarket daily to buy food. Cringing inside, he ignored his sterile instinct and always selected a trolley from the car park area before they had been cleaned and touched his face. Stood as close as possible to the other shoppers, deliberately picking up any item he had seen put back down, touched face. Hands on the check-out counter, touched face, push card machine buttons, touched face. Each assault on the government guidelines was like his own going over the top of the trenches moment, a willing foot soldier for the germ warfare, his personal paranoia the formidable enemy. How he screamed inside his head as he tore down hygiene barriers built up over five miserable decades and forced his hands and feet to obey. He was attentive to every surface within reach as he returned home, sliding his palms across like a kid collecting snow in winter.

Once home, he set the bag down in the kitchen and put the kettle on. Cups in his toxic hands, he carried them into the living room and set them down in front of his elderly parents. Like all dutiful sons, he kissed his mother and wiped the loose hair away from the side of her face. He held his father's hand tightly and reminded him once more about the lockdown rules, the modern world confusing him at the best of times. Shielded by the trust placed upon him, he made sure he spread his microscopic guests further as he continued to be their sole carer during this restricted period.

He had done his time, both at work and at home, and he would not miss this chance of parole and early release. The disease blown in from the east was changing the world, and he was no exception. It wouldn't be long before his parents needed more specialist care, more expensive care, to sell the house and his inheritance to pay for it care. All he was really doing was opening the door and letting vengeful mother nature do her bit, a natural ending of life, a blessed release for them all. Of course, he wouldn't be able to attend their funerals, but then that would be more money saved towards early retirement. Not such a bitter pill to swallow in the long run.

At the end of the fourth week, relieved to be feeling below par, Brian had developed an irritating cough and was pleased to see his temperature rise above one hundred by the evening. He was damn right suffering in the days following, but dutifully continued to look after his parents.

Ignoring the increasing discomfort he found himself in, Brian searched desperately for signs of its transference to his charges. Past any attempt at subtlety, he coughed into their faces, restrained himself from washing his hands and showed them more affection than he had in years. He left their unwashed clothes, the dirty bed sheets, and God help him, he even licked their food before he carried it through on trays. Yet they remained the same, eating, drinking and watching TV. No hint of infection. Neither worse nor better. Confusion grew within him as he painfully tended to them and searched despairingly for signs of success. An unforgiving mistress. The disease bit down harder on his lungs and much later than he should have done, he rang for an ambulance through rasping breaths as his worried parents looked on.

Plastic tubes, coloured lights and masks blurred his vision as the hospital staff fought to save him. Pain wracked his slender body and his lungs burnt fiercely, hot lava boiling over. Still, he smiled to himself in the infrequent moments of clarity that it was worth it to get what he wanted, knowing his parents could not possibly survive everything he was going through. They commented the smile on his lips on when they finally turned off the ventilator after he had drawn his last tormented breath, kindly mentioning it to his mother when they rang to tell her the bad news.

Unfortunately, his parents could not attend his simple, inexpensive funeral despite displaying none of the associated symptoms, and Brian didn't have to return to work after all.

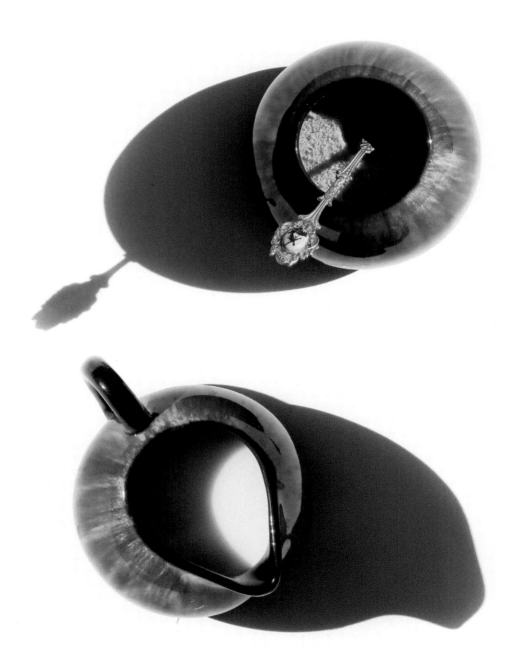

Netheravon Road

BY *EILEEN J ROBINSON*

"Gooooood morning,
Grenville Corner!
Suzanne Jarvis here on this
B-E-A-utiful morning.

"We hope you're enjoying
those bright blue skies out
there, and can you believe
this is our last bank holiday
before Christmas?"

DOROTHY NORTH SAT IN A ROCKER ON HER PORCH, listening to the wireless as a cup of tea steamed beside her. Her husband, Orson, clattered a grass cutter back and forth on their stretch of emerald lawn. The rain of the past week had finally broken, leaving the bushes diamond-dotted, and the puddles on the pavement shining with sun.

As Suzanne's familiar voice lilted from the wireless, the occupants of Netheravon Road bustled.

"—sure a lot of you will be heading on out to the beaches and parks to soak up the sun; we're all very jealous here in the studio. Don't you wish you were outside, Stuart? He's nodding, folks. Make the most of that sunshine for us. And for those of you heading out this afternoon, here's Harley Milner with your local travel updates. It's 9.07."

Bank holidays saw the residents of the road pour forth from their homes to tackle all the little jobs for which the weekends were never long enough. The Amberson twins, Elizabeth and Edward, emerged from number 50 with a bucket of soapy water and a sponge each. They washed the windows of their parents' house while their three dogs sunbathed. Dorothy often saw the two youngsters pottering about, keeping the house and garden spick and span. Filial dedication in the young pleased Dorothy.

"—currently backed up along the A406 due to a car accident in the early hours of this morning. A man and woman are confirmed as having died at the scene, and the area has been closed off, so alternative routes are—"

The Newells at number 52, Liam and Nora, knelt and tended to their sprawling flowerbeds, while their three young children sat crammed onto the front step and played hangman on the paving with white chalk. Nora's roses were the secret envy of Dorothy, who could no longer kneel to do her own weeding, but whose front garden had blossomed into a foam of wildflowers that was the secret envy of Nora.

Next to the Newell house, on the drive of number 54, stood Eilish and Donal, the young newlyweds, washing their car. Their two cats basked on their dandelion-spotted lawn, their dubious eyes locked on the stream from the hose. The couple had been at work when Dorothy emerged from her house that morning; their vigour gratified her. To her mind, young couples these days were so often layabouts. The Braithwaites of number 30, for instance.

"—believed to be from the Grenville area and were travelling alone in their car. No other motorists were involved in the incident, but police are asking for eye witnesses with any information to please come forward."

Sandra and Paul Braithwaite had embarked on yet another sojourn at the end of the last week. Their house stood dark and empty. While their neighbours' houses and gardens gleamed and flourished, the Braithwaites' curtains were closed, their drive vacant, and their lawn unkempt. What kind of example was that to set? Had they no pride? Perhaps if they spent less money swanning around, and more time on Netheravon Road ... Dorothy shook her head. Never mind. As long as there were young people, like Eilish, Donal, Elizabeth, and Edward, the future couldn't be too bleak.

After all, it was Donal who trimmed and pruned Dorothy and Orson's bushes every month, and never accepted a penny for his efforts. It was the Amberson boy, Edward, whom Dorothy spotted late in the evenings, walking back from number 46 and swinging a bag of garden tools by his knees. Celeste Wong's husband was often away for work and, with a newborn to mind, she needed help around the house. In return, Celeste allowed Edward to practice his gardening skills on her flowerbeds. Being a late addition to the road, the Amberson house had no back garden but looked out onto the cemetery of the church in the next avenue. The boy had green fingers, and Dorothy had heard that Celeste's back garden now boasted a rockery and dancing dahlias. She'd also heard that Edward was working on installing a pond; a rare young man—and only fourteen.

Orson's grass cutter clattered. The Amberson twins shrieked as they flicked suds at each other and watered the roots of the elms from their bucket. The Newell children drew imagined worlds on the pavement, their laughter bright as glitter on the breeze. Eilish and Donal hosed down their car, which sent pinkish grey water swirling into the gutters where it gurgled into the dark and out of sight.

"—advised to avoid the congestion in the Grenville area. Ring Road clockwise is moving, but delays anti-clockwise are expected until late this

afternoon. That's this morning's updates, folks. I'm Harley Milner, wishing you a great bank holiday wherever you are. Now, back to Suzanne.

Dorothy saw Eilish and Donal toss their sponges into an orange bucket and put an arm around each other. Donal kissed Eilish's head as they paced a circle around the gleaming car.

"You missed a bit," Dorothy called.

The young couple turned. Dorothy waved. They waved back, smiled, then linked hands and strode back towards their house, their cats gambolling after them. Dorothy watched the couple go. From the distance, beyond the road, came the incessant honks of car horns.

The world moved too fast for itself these days. Everyone was in such a hurry they had no time to respect their fellow man, nor keep up appearances. But when a bank holiday brought neighbours from their houses to complete the necessities of respectable living – washing the car, cleaning the windows, tending the flowerbeds – things weren't so bad. No matter what horrors went on in the outside world, Dorothy had this haven of order and respectability on Netheravon Road, where Nora's garden at 52 bloomed, the Amberson's windows at 50 sparkled, and the car of number 54 shone.

Dorothy sipped her steaming tea, leaned back in her rocker, and listened to the weather forecast. Nothing but sunshine expected.

Eilish and Donal stood at their kitchen sink and peered through the pretty, red-trimmed net curtain of their kitchen window. They could see Granny North on her porch where she rocked like a madwoman and chugged tea from a silver samovar.

"Do you think she saw something?" asked Eilish.

Donal shook his head. "Old dear's blind as a mole. Bits of them could've been stuck to the bonnet, and she couldn't have seen."

"People will notice when they don't come back."

"And we'll be just as concerned as everyone else on the road when that happens. Don't worry, my love. Everything's fine."

Eilish and Donal went about their day. They fed their cats. They made fruit salad. They basked in the sunshine on the road and drank chilled white wine with their neighbours in a toast to the last bank holiday before Christmas. On the drive outside their house, their car gleamed.

THE BAR FLY

BY ASHA BOOTH

"Imagine looking at someone and thinking
the rest of your life just isn't enough."

I followed his gaze to the couple sat by the
window. Their hands were knitted together,
and a glow of love seemed to radiate from
the slither of space between them...

THAT WAS THE SECOND TIME he had spoken since he arrived half an hour ago. The first was to order 'his usual' and I had fumbled for a moment before he clocked I was new and asked for a Guinness.

Though I'd never served him before, I knew he was a barfly, always stopping the other waiters from closing the bar while he chatted away about something or other. I'd been told he lived alone, and I felt a pang of guilt as I kept my head down and focused on the glasses.

"Bet you wouldn't believe it but I used to be like that." The couple's voices were just a low chatter, lips resting close to ears, as if they knew they were being watched.

"In love."

Even though I could only see his face in profile, I could hear the smile in his voice; lowered to match the whispers of the couple as if this was our secret.

"Used to be?"

We caught eyes for the first time since I poured his pint. "That came out wrong. I think love isn't something that you can ever really fall out of."

I laughed and thought of all the people that would surely disagree with that statement, myself included.

"I know what you're thinking. What would I know about that old guy like me? But I have been there." As he turned back to face them, a sense of longing laced his words.

"She was prettier than her. And I was better looking than him." He turned back to me with a wink and smiled. I watched the lines on his face rise and fall into place. Like creases on fresh linen sheets.

"When I first met her, she was younger than me. She was 15, and I was 18 and her Dad hated me. Couldn't understand why she wanted to be with me. He was a navy man and I remember the first time I met him it terrified me. Stood on the doorstep shaking like a shitty dog. You would have thought I was waiting for the Queen to open the door. He looked me up and down and it was so silent I could almost hear the cogs turning in his mind. Then her little sister, Jean, popped her head round the door frame. Tiny little thing. She can't have been over 5 and says bold as brass, "Polly told me you've got a tattoo?" That was it. He slammed the door in my face. Frightened me half to death."

He laughed, clearly remembering how that moment had felt.

They propped him up against the bar, but I could still tell he was tall. Well dressed. Wearing a light grey shirt with a few buttons undone at the top. His eyes, a piercing blue.

"On our first date we went out dancing. That was what us old people did back in those days. And none of that ridiculous stuff you see on the telly nowadays. We danced properly. I hate to brag, but we made quite a great pair. Jive was always our favourite." Looking off again, he seemed lost, rapping his fingers on the bar as if he could still hear the music now.

"Anyway," he shook his head, falling back to reality. "I spent the entire night trying to build up the courage to ask to kiss her, but I kept getting lost in her eyes. How corny! When I finally did, she laughed, put her hand on the back of my neck and pulled me close, whispering 'Only if you agree to a second date!' God, I think I fell in love with her right then and there."

He paused and took a quick sip from his pint. His words caught in his throat and his eyes were welling up. A single tear slipped over his cheek as he pushed his hand deep into his pocket, pulling out his wallet. He retrieved a small piece of paper, crinkled and slightly discoloured and, with a sigh, passed it to me.

I looked at the paper, then at him, waiting for some kind of explanation; or maybe even his blessing to open it. But his eyes were glued to his pint, which he was now spinning gently in his hand. Inside the paper read;

> *'I once heard*
> *That when you meet the love of your life*
> *The world freezes*
> *Time stops.*
> *But with you*
> *It was like someone lent on fast forward*
> *Everything seemed to fly by*
> *The moments turning to minutes and months*
> *Till suddenly I realised we were running out of time.*
> *If nothing else all this has made me realise*
> *Just how perfect every second has been with you.*
> *I promised you the rest of my life that night*

And I've kept my end of the bargain
I'm just sorry we didn't have longer, my dear.
But I promise wherever I end up
I'll be waiting
Waiting for the most perfect moment of my life.
But take as long as you need,
Don't rush on my account
Because I'll love you,
Now and forever.'

Silence. For the first time that evening, I noticed how still the bar was. The couple we had been watching had packed up and left and, with the two of us fallen silent, the pub had an eerie feel. Sunday evenings were always quiet, but it felt different. It was as if even the surrounding air was holding its breath and biting back tears.

I took in a breath, not wanting my voice to shake. "It's so beautiful." I folded it back up gently, following the original lines and slid it across the bar to him. For a moment I thought about how strange it is that such a small piece of paper seems to hold their entire relationship, their love and her life in its tender grasp. That piece of paper was his everything.

He sighed again, "She used to write a lot, but when she became ill, she said she just didn't feel creative anymore. It was only when I was cleaning out her room that I noticed this tucked under her pillow. I love it because it reminds me of that young girl I took out dancing. So full of love and life." His voice trembled. "I like her up there, just as she was when we first met, waiting for me. It's nice to know that she's not in pain anymore."

We both fell silent, him basking in Polly finally being at peace.

"She used to press flowers into books. Lovely idea really, but she used to forget where she'd put them. So sometimes, even to this day, when I open a book I get a lap full of old daisies or forget-me-nots. Maybe she knew it would make me laugh. Her way of making me smile, even when she wasn't around to do it herself." He wiped his cheek, and with it the final tear that was caught in his eyelash. His eyes seemed bluer now than before, kinder even. I guess now he'd told me about his life, his soul seemed to shine through a little more.

"We had so many happy years together and I sometimes feel silly for wasting a single second of it. We got longer than most, so I shouldn't complain. But when you picture growing old with someone, you do feel slightly short changed."

With that the small glass wash machine gave a last sigh and pinged signalling she was finished for the evening, which dragged us both back to reality. He lifted the sleeve of the arm resting on the bar and glimpsed his watch.

"God is that the time?" he laughed, "You must be sick of me by now! Polly did always say I could talk the ears off of anyone."

Little did he know that I would often think back to that night; to our chat and to the story he'd told me. And every time I thought of them both on that dance floor, with tears pricking my eyes, I would pray that there is something after this world where they can be reunited at last.

"Well, I best be getting home, the dog will wonder where I am." He pulled on his jacket and made his way over to the door. Before reaching for the handle, he turned and called back to me, "Thank you for a lovely evening. Hopefully, I will see you in here again soon."

He turned his collar up, and just like that he slipped out into the darkness.

SPEARS OF IRONY

BY ALAN PEAT

My husband
and best friend,
Geoffrey Anderson,
died as a result of
climate change...

WE'D BOTH MET WHILE STUDYING for a degree in zoology at Leeds University. We also came out together, or rather I did, for Geoff's own parents were a little more in tune with the times than Betty and Norman Prentice. A little more understanding, perhaps. My family also weren't big on hugging or kissing, or even comfortable sharing their innermost feelings with others. My sexuality was therefore more a cross to bear rather than an opportunity to be recognised, for whom I really am. Geoff helped me change all that.

After graduating, I found employment as a biology teacher at a local secondary school. My boyfriend joined a research institute specialising in the ecological effects, of what eventually came to be termed 'climate change', on the natural world. This took him to some of the remotest parts of our planet, and I was fortunate enough to accompany him on some of those overseas trips; South America, the rainforests of Borneo and the Great Barrier Reef to name but a few.

Our combined love of nature spilled over into our domestic life; two springer spaniels named Charles and Darwin and a stray ginger cat called Marmalade. We were comfortable both financially and emotionally, our gay marriage a stable relationship that, but for the fact we were both males, bordered on the straight. Neither of us bathed in the bright neon light of Gay Pride, or wore rainbow coloured socks to display our allegiance to a world of protest and often pointless gestures of exhibitionism. We had earned our equality but didn't feel the need to rub other peoples' faces in it.

I was listening to one of our favourite pieces of music, Grieg's Peer Gynt Suite, when the phone rang, that call from overseas which informed me in tones of subdued reverence that Geoff had been involved in an accident; a fatal accident. I remember slumping onto the sofa, shaking from head to foot, overcome with disbelief. Real grief, the type one has to come to terms with, would take its natural course. Spending the rest of our lives together had been a modest ambition on cruelly curtailed through ironic circumstances. Aase's Death emanated from the speakers.

The UK Arctic Research Station is on the west coast of the island of Spitsbergen. This is an outpost of Norway one thousand miles above the Arctic Circle. I flew to Oslo first and then switched planes to the tiny airport of Longyearbyen. This was a world like no other.

The actual research station on is in a remote place called Ny-Alesund, and is only open from March through to September. Another fortnight and Geoff would have been home.

I was met by one of my husband's work colleagues, a smart young woman called Agnes, who tried to take my mind off things by pointing out various items of interest as we travelled the last forty miles of my journey. She must have found it awkward meeting me in such circumstances. But Geoff's body had to be formally identified before the coroner could release his body back to the UK.

"We're nearer to Greenland than Norway," she shouted as she flung the Toyota LandCruiser around a tight bend.

I looked out of the side window at the distant snow-covered mountains, harsh in their uncompromising ability to make one feel hemmed in. This was a hostile environment, and although the hard earth and sparse vegetation on gave the illusion of a more temperate landscape, I could visualise what it would look like in winter.

"Do you ever see the Northern Lights?" I asked.

"The Aurora Borealis," she whispered and took her eyes off the road for a moment to look at me. "I have seen it occasionally, but the best me to witness the spectacle is during the winter months."

I turned to her. "It was always Geoff's ambition for us to see it together." There was a lengthy pause.

"I'm so sorry for your loss," and just for a moment I thought she might cry.

I identified Geoff's body. I stared at his lifeless face laying on that slab of stainless steel. Thank God that his handsome features had escaped the cruelties of his death. I was reliably informed that any significant injuries inflicted on his body were thankfully covered by a shroud.

"It's the food they're after," Doctor Svenson told me as he wiped his glasses and led me out of the temporary morgue. "Polar bears are having a pretty rough time of it of late."

His comments provided very few crumbs of comfort. I would have spent more me with my husband's body but a sense of obligation on towards the etiquette of good manners found me following in the wake of the dour Norwegian.

I realised that even in the presence of death I wasn't a hugger. My need to be physically sick only exacerbated my restrained sense of grief. I excused myself and visited the nearest toilet.

"What did the doctor mean when he said that Polar bears were having a rough time of it?" I asked Agnes over two very large vodkas.

"Global warming is affecting their natural habitat. The gradual melting of the ice cap is reducing their hunting grounds. Added to that is the fact that the bears' major source of food, the seal, are moving themselves to find new feeding grounds." She paused, sank her drink, and stared at me. "Everything in nature is connected."

I tapped the side of my glass and looked around this very spartan hut. "Where was Geoff when it attacked him?"

"Near to here."

I swallowed the fiery spirit. "Don't you protect yourselves from wild animals?"

She nodded and poured us both another generous shot. "If you go offsite, you have to be accompanied by a colleague and carry a rifle with you at all times. Geoff had been trained in the use of these firearms. But..."

"But what?"

"Polar bears are becoming scavengers. That's what we humans are turning them into." She thumped the tabletop with her fist. "First, we bugger up their natural environment and then we leave our garbage out for them to sift through. For some animals, it's become easier than hunting."

I put my head into my hands. Then I chuckled and looking at Agnes sitting there in her brightly patterned sweater. "So my husband was killed by one of the very creatures he was trying to protect," and smiled at the way providence can some times disregard happiness and instead throw spears of bitter irony our way.

Three months later I visited my sister in Manitoba, Canada, and together we scattered my husband's ashes under the spectral, shimmering waves of the Northern Lights.

The Last Dragon

BY MATTHEW TANSINI

NORTHUMBRIA

They had travelled at dawn,
only resting when the sun
dipped below the horizon. As
they flew, unnatural storms
had howled across the
landscape below...

Now night had fallen, and Luthren sat staring into the fire, aching, his travelling cloak wrapped around him against the chill. Nathir lurked at the very edge of the fire's light, blanketed by his own wings, his great crested head resting on the ground. His scales glittered like lost jewels.

They had left the crumbling ruins of their village days ago, travelling vaguely south. All they left behind were the burial mounds of those the plague had taken. Luthren kept hoping for some sign, some portent from the Gods that he was doing the right thing. So far they had been sullen and silent. Perhaps they were dead too, now they no longer had anyone to worship them.

Suddenly, Nathir sat up. His eyes narrowed, and a low rumble began in his throat. Luthren shushed the beast, murmuring quiet instructions. Nathir looked back at him for a moment, his eyes inscrutable. And then, with surprising deftness, his great bulk melted away into the blackness.

After a few minutes, someone came into the paltry circle of firelight. A young man, dressed in a monk's habit. Luthren regarded him warily. There was nothing in his pack worth stealing, but desperate times made men do strange things.

The monk looked just as uneasy as Luthren. He was young, barely more than a teenager, and had a gaunt, starved look to him – one common to the poor folk of the islands. He was shivering.

After a few moments, Luthren nodded, and the monk sat down gratefully, shuffling close to the fire and warming his hands. Luthren watched him in silence a few moments more, then turned back to the flames.

"I've not seen any warriors like you before." The monk said.

"How do you know I'm a warrior?" Luthren replied. The monk indicated the blade at his belt.

"Strange armour too," he said, gesturing. Luthren glanced down at the polished, scaled hide he wore, decorated with intricate looping patterns.

"I'm not a warrior." He said.

"If you're not a warrior, then what are you?" the monk asked. Luthren considered this.

"I don't know." He admitted.

A sudden breeze disturbed the dust at their feet, and the fire flickered. In the air above them, Luthren caught the barest glimpse of green as Nathir skimmed overhead.

"Are you a Christian?" The monk asked. Luthren shook his head. "Then what do you believe in?"

"I'm not sure." Luthren said. "Everyone who believed as I did is dead.'

The monk considered this briefly, before another sound drew their attention. Multiple footsteps,heavy and urgent. The monk's face drained of what little colour it had.

"I thought I had lost them." He whispered. "I have nothing to give. Oh, Lord, preserve me."

"You are a holy man." Luthren pointed out.

"You think they care about that?"

"Can't your god protect you?"

The monk gave Luthren a withering look.

Three figures stepped into the light of the fire; big, brawny men clad in ragged clothes, with wild hair and dark eyes. They carried crude, vicious clubs made of splintered wood and decorated with dark stains.

The monk scrambled to his feet and backed away from the men, his hands raised before him as if in surrender. Luthren remained seated.

"Mind if we join you?" the leader of the trio leered humourlessly. The thugs moved closer, their weapons loose and ready.

"Do something!" the monk hissed at Luthren. The traveller cast him a tired glance. "Maybe it would be best if you moved on." He said to the men, his voice calm.

The leader looked at him for a moment, and then laughed, hacking and phlegmatic. He turned and spat contemptuously. Luthren wrinkled his nose.

"Brave one, eh?" The bandit said. "Makes no difference to me."

Luthren sighed quietly and stood, wincing as his tired limbs protested. Each of the men was easily a head taller than him.

There was another gust from overhead, and the fire guttered and crackled.

The bandits attacked, but Luthren was already moving. He stepped forward, slipping between them as they lunged in unruly union. He turned and drew his weapon in one smooth movement. His blade flashed, and one of his attackers gave a broken howl and fell to his knees, his hamstrings cut. In a practised motion, Luthren swiftly reached round and slit his throat.

The other two rounded and came again. Luthren ducked and weaved, but their ferocity drove him back. His foot slipped as a glancing blow struck his left shoulder. His attacker grinned, but then there was a sudden hard thunk from behind him, and the man's features went slack. He drunkenly staggered sideways, dropping his club and clutching at his head. Luthren punched his blade through the brute's throat. The man's eyes bulged and his mouth opened for a breath that never came, and then he fell, twitching, into a widening pool of his own blood. Luthren looked up. The monk stood before him, grasping a log from the fire, its end still smouldering.

Suddenly, a fierce blow sent Luthren flying. He landed on his back; the wind knocked out of him. Head spinning, he tried to rise, but the bandit leader stood over him, his club raised in both hands.

Suddenly, the fire flickered and dance wildly, and the surrounding dust shifted and hissed in a fierce blast of wind. High above, flame seared the night sky.

A moment later Nathir fell to earth, landing with an earth shattering crash behind Luthren. He reared up to his full height and let loose a great, shrieking roar that echoed around them in the night.

The bandit's cudgel fell from numb fingers as he stood and stared at Nathir, dumbstruck. The beast snarled and smashed him aside with a single blow. The bandit's broken form vanished into the blackness, and a second later there was a dull thud as his corpse fell to earth.

Nathir turned on the monk who was still clutching his smoking log. The young man fell to his knees in terror, but Luthren scrambled to his feet and staggered between them.

"Enough!" he shouted.

Nathir snarled and snapped, claws digging into the earth, his tail whipping back and forth. But Luthren stood his ground.

"Enough."

Nathir looked at his master, his aggression ebbing away. The traveller reached forwards and clapped his flank in thanks. The beast turned, grumbling as he resumed his vigil at the fire's edge.

"What is it?" the monk whispered hoarsely. He was still on his knees.

Luthren hauled him to his feet. He looked at the creature and smiled sadly.

"The last of his kind."

Ealdred awoke and lay still for a few moments. His dreams were fading, leaving half-memories of fire and blood. The storm that had battered the monastery throughout the night had mercifully passed, and all was quiet around him. Since his return from the pilgrimage, he had thrown himself into his duties with renewed vigour, as though that might cleanse him of what he had seen and done that night.

When he had awoken the next morning, shivering in the mist, he had been alone. But as he looked around, he noticed something lying by the embers of the fire, something emerald green. It was a single scale; leathery, tough, and as large as his palm.

Ealdred knew they should punish him for his sins, but some animal instinct of self-preservation made him keep his silence. Times were tough, and people were starving. If he spoke of what had happened, he could be banished. And so, however much he despised himself for it, Ealdred kept the truth to himself.

Suddenly there were shouts from the main hall. Ealdred dressed quickly and hastened there. Several men were already crowded around the narrow window, pointing and murmuring. He joined them, craning his neck to see into the bay beyond.

At first he saw nothing, just the grey sea under an endless mass of sullen clouds. Then he spotted the long ships approaching from the horizon, their patterned sails fluttering in the wind as they drew nearer.

"They're coming from the East." Brother Cynwulf murmured. "No-one sails from the East."

"It's another portent!" someone else cried.

Ealdred said nothing. All he could think about was the traveller and the beast in the dark, its eyes glowing red in the firelight. He turned his own eyes skyward, listening for the beating of approaching wings.

Extract from The Anglo-Saxon Chronicle for the year 793 A.D.:

"Horrible portents came over the land of Northumbria, terrifying the people: there were immense flashes of lightening, and we saw fiery dragons flying in the air. A great famine followed; and shortly after, the ravaging of wretched heathen men devastated and destroyed God's church in Lindisfarne."

THE RAVEN

BY *AMANDA KEARSEY*

Keeping his foot hard on the pedal, the classic
BMW bounced and grated along the twisting
country road. Alex was late and lost...

HE SLAPPED THE STEERING WHEEL in frustration, angry with himself. Weak winter light flickered intermittently through the tunnel of trees as he sped along, but he didn't notice the shuffling figure at the side of the road.

Until he hit it.

A sickening crunch as the impact reverberated through the steering wheel and into his shoulders, flinging him backwards. The shocking glimpse of a body flung against his windscreen before rolling back down the bonnet.

Slamming hard on the brakes, he sat shocked, hands shaking, before jumping out of the car and running to the fallen body. An elderly woman in dirty, threadbare clothes, arms thrown outward like wings. Glass, dirt, and blood were intertwined in white, matted hair, fanning out like a halo.

"Oh no!" he breathed raggedly. "No, No!"

Her eyes were staring. Petrified, he waited for them to blink. They didn't.

Hesitantly, Alex he felt her wrist for a pulse. None. He gave a shocked sob. "Dead! No! You're dead ...you can't be!"

Kneeling back, Alex took a deep breath before shakily considering his options. He ought to call the police. But... what about his fast track career? He could lose everything.

Wiping a sweaty palm over his face, he looked at the BMW. It didn't seem too bad. A broken headlight, but that could be explained. Alex glanced back at the body. She was dead. That was, of course, sad, but there wasn't anything he could do about it, was there? Nevertheless, guilt gnawed at him.

"I'm sorry ..." he muttered as he pulled himself to his feet. He squared his shoulders resolutely. "But it's for the best." Scrutinising his tailored suit carefully, he brushed off dirt and twigs. No blood.

Checking up and down the road, he saw no one else. So, well. There it was. No witnesses.

Although, as he turned to leave, he stopped by a loud "Arrk!" that rendered the winter stillness. A large coal-black bird stalked up and down beside the body, examining him with a beady eye. A raven. Clever birds, his father had once said. People had taught them to talk, he'd told his son, even believed they were mystical creatures.

The bird stopped its pacing and glared at him.

Alex shifted uncomfortably under its judging scrutiny, but then picking up a stone, he furiously threw it at the bird. It hopped away, just out of reach, but didn't leave. He threw another and it did the same.

"Go away!" he yelled. But the bird refused to move. Giving up, he stalked back to the car.

The engine started up fine. Backing up from the body, he carefully manoeuvred past it, throwing a backward glance as he drove away. The raven was still there, watching.

A few stiff drinks in his local pub that evening did much to dispel his anxiety, softening the edges of his guilt. But he couldn't escape the news report blaring out of the pub's television. Tragic death of an elderly hit-and-run victim, no suspects so far. A known eccentric who lived alone, apart from a bizarre collection of caged wild birds. So sad. As the reporter did her bit to camera, he noticed his hands were shaking. More drinks solved that problem.

He breathed deeply, enjoying the cold reviving air that stung his face as he made his way home. Usually this part of town was quiet, but tonight, as he neared his house, he perceived that the trees were unusually alive with an agitated, rustling commotion. Disconcerted, he hurried to his front door, but stumbled, dropping his key. As he reached down to pick it up, he felt a winged something swoop over his head, its feathery tips stroking his neck. He shivered, whipping his head around wildly, but nothing was there. Probably, he reasoned nervously, just old leaves blowing in the breeze.

But a sudden feverish desire to get inside to safety overcame him. He frantically jiggled his key in the lock, pushing at the door until it gave, pitching him awkwardly into the dark interior. He quickly turned to slam the door shut, and with alarm, glimpsed the figure of a large, coal-black bird perched on the shrub behind him. It regarded him with an unnerving beady eye.

He hastily slammed the door shut.

Alcohol induced a heavy sleep. But shifting, potent dreams threw him awake at dawn. Lying tangled in sweaty sheets, he became conscious of birdsong outside his window. He wasn't a connoisseur of birdsong, but even to his ears, it sounded raucous in the early morning air.

He padded to the window, blinking the sleep out of his eyes, and threw back the curtains.

The bare trees outside his windows were filled with all types of wild birds, perched on every available branch. And steadily observing his bedroom window was the same raven from the night before. But it couldn't be, could it?

He nearly tore the curtains loose in his anxiety to shut out the birds.

Sleep being impossible, he padded downstairs for hot coffee and toast. A quick check on the internet provided a repair garage. The quicker he had the car fixed, the better–fewer people to notice his damaged car and therefore the fewer excuses he would have to make. He kept the kitchen blinds closed, though. The sight of the birds was unnerving, although he couldn't say why. Anxiety roiled around uncomfortably in his stomach, making the hot buttered toast taste like cardboard in his mouth. He threw it in the bin. The freshly brewed coffee didn't fare much better either.

After a quick shower which didn't do much to revive him, he unlocked the interior door to his garage and flicked on the light switch. The headlamp was a stark reminder of the accident, and Alex found he couldn't look at it too closely. Instead, he let his glance slide away from the incriminating evidence of his guilt.

Shivering in the chill morning air, he cautiously opened the garage doors and peered out. The birds were gone. His shoulders sagged in relief. But he was annoyed with himself; they were only birds, after all. He left the engine running and driver's door open while locking up the garage, then reversed down his short drive, making his way out of the town.

Several miles later, however, he had to admit that he was lost. The road ahead disappeared into a tunnel of twisted, bare-limbed trees, enclosing the lane in a gloomy tunnel. There was no signpost in sight. A growing sense of being watched had crept coldly up his spine as he drove. But there was no one following; no one to be seen at all. The feeling grew, stabbing uncomfortably into the back of his neck, and in sudden alarm, he realised the road was all too familiar. The same lane he had travelled yesterday. The site of the accident. Sweat broke out on his brow, his hands felt cold and clammy. He struggled to grip the now slippery steering wheel as the car bounced on the uneven road.

A rustling, flapping sound in the back seat nearly made him loose his grip altogether. The wheel spun, and he grabbed hold of it, glancing frantically in the mirror.

A large coal-black bird jumped onto the headrest of his seat. "Hello!" The raven squawked into his ear.

"Agghh!" he yelled in shock. The car wobbled dangerously.

The raven flapped its wings in annoyance.

"Get out!" screamed Alex, hitting the window button open. The wind rushed furiously into the speeding car.

Unperturbed, the Raven hopped down onto the passenger seat, one beady eye observing Alex, before jumping up and down, almost gleefully. "You're dead." it croaked.

The car hit a bump, and Alex felt it spin wildly out of his control. Hitting the brakes hard, he couldn't stop the car's momentum as it veered towards a large oak tree.

He was powerless to avoid the oncoming impact. The windscreen shattered into myriad pieces, while the bonnet crumpled, pinning him to his seat. Screeching noisily, the raven escaped the wreckage through the open window.

But Alex watched it go through sightless eyes. Unaware of the oncoming rain as it spattered through the open window. Unaware of another car pulling up, a shocked driver rushing to help.

In a satisfied dance, the raven observed the scene from the oak tree above. Its beady eye glinted in the weak winter light.

"Sorry!" it croaked, before launching itself into the wintry sky.

BENEATH THE GLASS

BY *GRACE BUFFHAM*

Before the water swallowed the Earth, my brother Tom spent one long summer crafting me the most beautiful walnut, glass-bottomed boat...

IT WAS THE SUMMER of a terrible drought, where our desert-stranded house almost collapsed from the heat. Yet Tom insisted that the sea would come, and we needed to be prepared. He was right like he always was, but I couldn't imagine that the dry sand that so often burnt water would someday consume my feet.

I remember little of where we lived at that time, but even then, there were no other people, it was always just Tom and I. We spent most of the time reserving energy, quietly sweating, in the make-shift house that Tom built. He would brave the coldest – yet still swelteringly hot – part of the day to work on the boat. Sometimes, before my bedtime, he would let me watch as he expertly sawed, planed, and sanded the course tree stump until it became as smooth as skin. It allowed me to help with some small parts: cutting and sanding bits of wood. Tom would gratefully receive my butchered and mangled parts, always breathing life into them.

Other times, the cool part of the day was reserved for finding food. There was little vegetation, but lots of debris which Tom said was a hotbed for hidden treasures. Our meals came in dust covered cans and bits of plastic, and then, once we had scraped every morsel from them, we would turn the cans into targets and try to bowl them down with rocks. Tom was good at finding fun.

I would relish the times when he would tell me stories about the world, about all the places and people that didn't exist anymore. I would ask questions with an insatiable thirst for knowledge. I'd ask about the machines that destroyed us from the inside, and the asteroids that came, and the bombs that exploded, and how the earth got hotter, and caused the floods and famine and disease. But most of all, I asked him about the people. He would tell me how they lived in little boxes and had jobs that were never completed so they had to return each day, and how they invented things for comfort, not survival like TVs and dishwashers and socks. The most fascinating part was that there were families like us, but with mums and dads, and communities; filled with partners, friends, and people of all different kinds. He told me how all of them came together amidst the fear and horror when all the bad started happening, but how it was too late to fix it. I wanted to know if there were any other people left and if we could find them – Tom didn't know. Eventually, after many persistent questions, Tom said only when the boat was complete would he answer them.

Eventually he presented it to me, and I beamed at him with pride. I marvelled at the smooth curve of the bow jutting out, bringing the two sides of the boat together like an embrace. There were even intricately carved flourishes blinking on the hull. Yet as beautiful as it was, I later discovered, the secret beauty of the boat was that it held within it all the knowledge of the universe.

Then the day came, like my brother had said, when the desert sand saturated with water beneath our feet, and our house slowly sank into the earth. We gathered our supplies and pushed the boat out onto the water, never to return to the land again.

The first time he asked the boat a question, I thought the sea air had got to him. He called out to the boat, "Glass- bottomed boat, tell me what 'majestic' is."

And to my surprise, the bottom of the boat lit up as if by magic, shimmering translucent, and the blackness of the sea transformed into dolphins swimming in synchrony.

That is when I discovered the boat had the power to answer any worldly question you could imagine. It was utterly captivating. With a simple question, the glass-bottomed boat showed us wonders upon wonders. It entertained us and kept us hopeful while we clung on for life through storms and food shortages.

When I said "Glass-bottomed boat, show me what 'beauty' is.", the glass would reveal to us, fiery tailed fishes, swarms of sardine constellations and the rainbow coloured city of anemones on the tranquil ocean floor.

Tom had a knack for deciphering the meanings which I soon learnt for myself, but even then, sometimes the answer it gave was vague and confusing.

"Are humans good?" I asked.

And there would appear thousands of fish in different colours, some eating the smaller fish, some being chased in a flurry of activity.

We saw many wonders at sea, learning about this unknown world together, but the old world that Tom told me about was not forgotten. Our boat became a plane to the old, sunken world. When we found ourselves over the sunken cities, we would weave around the tops of bottomless skyscrapers that peaked out above the all-consuming black water.

Then one day after the boat had swum us out of a more hazardous sunken city, I asked the ultimate question "Glass- bottomed boat, tell me where are the people?"

But all the glass -bottomed boat showed me was an endless and bottomless expanse of dark swirling water.

I would come back for days finding alternative ways to ask the question;

"Where did they go? How can I find them?"

I would pace around the glass waiting for something to change and pound my fist against the glass, staring at my reflection, but still, nothing changed. Tom warned me to let it go, to accept the unknown, but I didn't want to listen.

The last time I visited the glass, we were being tossed amid a storm like a leaf in the wind. My anger was bubbling like the furious wild sea that was swarming around us.

"Where did the people go?" I shouted.

Suddenly, I saw something change in the glass, a flicker of a shape.

I turned to my brother to show him there was something in the water, but he was nowhere to be seen. Then, looking through the glass, I realised beneath the boat was not an answer, it was my brother struggling for his life.

I tried to save him. I jumped under and pulled him out, but the tendrils of seaweed had already ripped the skin on his neck like a grotesque necklace. I just remember his deep blue eyes, as empty as the ocean.

I never asked the boat another question after that.

Now I'm sitting on the edge of the boat, staring at the vast ocean. The lulling water gently licked my feet. I don't know how much time has passed since the screaming and the crying, and the eventual calming of the storm. I am staring blankly out to the sea, there's nothing else for me to do. I feel as though I am trapped on this murderous boat that I once thought was our salvation.

Breaking my silence, I ask for the last time, "Glass-bottomed boat, where are the people?"

I don't really expect an answer, I'm just hoping this time it will take me. But it doesn't.

I continue gazing blankly, letting the seconds tick by, the thought of escape growing stronger inside me. Suddenly my attention is brought back to reality by a glint of light out of the corner of my eye.

I immediately draw my gaze to it. I see a small black dot on the horizon, that I am reluctant to believe, appears to be getting bigger. I rub my weathered knuckles into my eyes. The more I focus on the dot, the more I'm sure it's coming closer. But it's not until I can fully recognise the corporeal shape that I can say to myself, there undeniably is a large boat coming towards me. I wonder who could be on it.

THE PRINCESS'S HAND
BY GORDON ADAMS

Like many a folk story, this
particular tale features a cast of
characters including a King, his
beloved daughter (the Princess)
and a host of suitors who are
seeking the Princess's hand
in marriage.

WE BEGIN THIS STORY on the Princess's eighteenth birthday...The Princess was a true romantic. Her heart was set on finding the lover of her dreams: someone who was courageous and intelligent. The King wanted his daughter to be happy more than anything else on earth. He was also, like many fathers, just a little protective of his daughter. Now that his daughter had come of age, he didn't want to her to marry just any old Prince Tom, Prince Dick or Prince Harry. (Particularly not Prince Harry). Therefore, being a wise and sensible King, he devised a series of tests: three tests which any suitor would need to pass, to win his daughter's hand in marriage.

The first test was a test of courage: to swim or wade across a lake filled with piranha fish – man-eating fish – and retrieve a golden goblet from an island in the middle of that lake. It was a test which only the most courageous would attempt.

The second test was a test of strength: to hold a giant boulder aloft from the setting of the sun to the crowing of the cockerel the following morning. This was a feat that would defeat all but the strongest suitor.

The third test was a test of intelligence: to choose an outfit for the princess, which would make her appear even more beautiful. As the Princess was already exquisite indeed (and, boy, did she know it) this was a challenge which would be formidable even for a self- confident suitor with an IQ as big as his ego.

Having devised these three tests, the King could finally sleep at nights knowing his daughter would only marry someone who possessed courage, strength and intelligence.

Now, the Princess was beautiful, charming and intelligent. She was also next in line to inherit a not inconsiderable kingdom. Thus, it was no surprise that suitors flocked from all around the world to seek her hand in marriage. But three long years later, as the Princess celebrated her twenty-first birthday, she was still unmarried. Over the intervening years, many Princes had tried and failed to pass these tests. The world's population of eligible Princes was becoming severely depleted and the piranha fish in the lake were growing smug and fat.

Just then, right on cue (and fortunately for our story) a young man turned up at the castle gates. He rapped firmly at the door. Rat-a-tat-tat! This man was dressed in a smart business suit and confidently announced he sought the Princess's hand in marriage.

"Well, are you a Prince?" asked the King, looking him up and down.

"No," said the man. "I am a businessman. A technology entrepreneur, no less. And I have come to seek your daughter's hand in marriage."

"Well, you can't!" replied the King. "You have to be a Prince."

"Nay, sire," said the businessman. "I think you will find otherwise. I am a global technology entrepreneur. My company employs the very best lawyers. How else do you think we could avoid paying all that Corporation Tax? My lawyers have studied your royal proclamation and nowhere does it say you have to be a Prince. Now then, rules are rules!"

After reflecting for a moment, the King had to admit he'd probably missed that bit out. Reluctantly, he agreed to let the businessman take the tests.

The next morning, the King, the Princess and the businessman gathered beside the lake for the first test: the test of courage. This test was, if you recall: to swim or wade across a lake filled with piranha fish and retrieve a golden goblet from the island in the middle of that lake. As they gathered by the side of the lake, the businessman suddenly pulled a keypad out from his pocket.

"As a businessman," he announced, "I know that success in business nowadays is through technology-led outsourcing and so I have outsourced these three challenges to my robot."

He pressed a large red button on the keypad. Everyone heard a loud clanking noise coming from afar. Finally, a large mechanical man appeared from over the hill. This robot immediately waded into the water and across to the lake. The piranha fish tried to bite him, but their teeth bounced off the hard metal of his legs. The robot retrieved the golden goblet from the island with ease and returned, clutching it aloft above his head.

The King was forced to declare the Businessman had passed the first test. Thus, they came to the second test which was, if you remember, the test of strength. (And if you don't remember, you really must try to pay attention–didn't your mother teach you anything?) The second test was to hold a giant boulder aloft from the setting of the sun to the crowing of the cockerel the following morning.

Well, on hearing the terms of this test, the robot scanned the lakeside and located the giant boulder. He reached down and effortlessly lifted that giant boulder above his head. At this point, he yawned and announced he was switching himself off till the following morning to conserve power. He powered down, still clutching the giant boulder aloft above his head. And that's how they found him the following morning, still holding the boulder aloft. The cockerel crowed, and the King admits the second test had also been passed with ease.

The time had come for the third and most challenging test: the test of intelligence. This test was, if you recall, to design an outfit for the Princess that would make her appear even more beautiful. The King whispered an instruction to the Princess to leave the gathering and return wearing the dress he had just bought her for her twenty-first birthday. This was a golden dress made from the finest silk and had to be found somewhere within the Kingdom.

She returned looking utterly stunning. Even the robot gasped.

"Look at my beautiful daughter," the King declared. "What could she wear that would make her appear even more beautiful?"

"Why, nothing!" replied the robot instantly, in a tone which suggested he was indeed smitten.

This was, whichever way you looked at it, the right answer, and either shows that robots are highly intelligent or that they possess a wicked sense of humour. The businessman hugged the robot and danced a jig of delight. The King had to admit that all three of his tests had been passed by the robot. "I am therefore offering my daughter's hand in marriage to... this robot."

"Hey, hang on a minute!" shouted the businessman. "That's not fair!"

"Rules are rules," said the King. "You can get your lawyers to confirm this for you."

The robot seized the remote control from the businessman and threw it into the lake.

"No need for that anymore," said the robot with a wink, as he and the Princess walked off hand-in-hand towards the sunset.

And they both lived happily ever after.

Now the moral to this thoroughly contemporary folk tale is this: 'Technology-led outsourcing in business is fine, right up until the day you find it's your role that's being outsourced to a robot.'

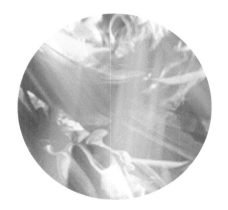

This compilation is available in Ebooks High 1 & 2
EBook High 3 : Best of the Rest stories

EBooks editions and Artist Prints
are all available to purchase over at
www.**HappyStoryStore.com**

Cover and inside Illustrations by:
Clare Newton FRSA
Editor: Michael Taylor
Art Editor: Louise Taylor
Typography: Louise Taylor
Publisher: Happy London Press
Printed by: Podww England

VERY SPECIAL THANKS

To all the amazing people who have helped make the High One
and Hi2020 short story competition a success.

Wycombe Sound 106.6 fm and Jonathan Pagden
Our Judge Manager: David Wolstenholme

5 Top Tier Judges:
Christopher Norris
Alexandra Ely
Sheryl Shurville
Jonathan Pagden
Andrew Segal

34 Pre Judges from around the UK
and Little Chalfont Community Library
Sheryl Shurville co-owner of Chiltern Bookshops
for hosting the hardback edition
and all the writers who took part.